FEARLESS HART

A CROSS CREEK SMALL TOWN NOVEL

KELLY COLLINS

BOOK NOOK PRESS

Cover design by Sly Fox

Edits by Show Me Edits

CHAPTER ONE

MIRANDA

I didn't drive the old back roads because they reminded me of where I'd grown up and memories I wasn't ready to face; memories I'd fled to Cross Creek to escape.

But the funny thing about the past is that it has a way of following no matter how far or fast you run.

My Tahoe's headlights danced as my tires hit three potholes, perfectly staggered to be impossible to miss.

"Damn it," I growled as my water bottle popped out of the cup holder to roll around on the passenger floor, well out of reach. Not that I'd be so irresponsible as to reach for it while I was driving.

I wouldn't even be on this bumpy-ass road if I hadn't received a report that someone was on an old farm out here. A neighbor called in a suspicious vehicle, and though there was little to no crime in Cross Creek, I still needed to check it out. Nothing got past the old folks in this town. They might have been deaf, but they heard everything; blind but somehow could see a trespasser from a mile away.

No doubt I'd probably just come across teens making out and send them on their way. I'd already heard from dispatch that Ethel tried to talk her ear off while making the call, and I smiled as I thought about the sweet old couple. Still, I breathed a sigh of relief that the call was over trespassers and not more drama from Benji, the town journalist, who took it upon himself to air everyone else's dirty laundry. Publishing that article about Kandra's personal life was just bad journalism counting on sensationalism, and it almost broke Kandra and Noah up.

Hitting the brakes, I waited for two deer who entered the road. They stopped mid-lane, staring at me before bolting across the street into the field's chest-high grass.

I watched them go while my thoughts wandered back to how Benji would get out of this trouble. Something about him set off my alarm bells a long time ago. But what he'd done to Kandra was downright predatory, and the entire town saw it and rallied behind her.

Just last week, there had been a town-wide baby shower for the mom-to-be, and she and Noah were guests of honor. Everyone showed up and brought more things than one child could ever use or need.

An event like that told me exactly what kind of town I lived in. On the flip side, Benji had found himself persona non grata. Even Roy booted him, which meant I could go to the bar for a beer to unwind without the nosy journalist bugging me for an interview.

"Good riddance." The sound of my voice echoed through the cab of the cruiser. "I don't want him digging into my past for dirt because my life is a damn landfill."

The old farmhouse loomed to my right, rising like an ethereal ghost through the layer of fog drifting in from the creek. A truck came into view, and I chuckled. Things were about to get more interesting. I hadn't stumbled upon kids making out after all.

My pulse was racing as I parked. Trying to steady it, I scooped my water bottle off the passenger floor and took a long drink before exiting my vehicle.

My eyes adjusted to the total darkness while I moved to the truck. Overhead, a billion stars shone like an impossible scattering of fairy lights. The moon added a silvery glow as my breath hung in mini clouds near my face.

The dark mixed with the night lit up by stars, and the left behind fog gave the whole place an almost spooky feel as I approached Bayden's form. That curious warmth he evoked in me didn't escape my notice, and I wondered if I was developing feelings because of how much we talked. I mean, he was part of the crew building the new police station. We consulted quite a lot, so the time we spent together would lead to a kind of closeness, right?

Maybe that was what I told myself to keep from panicking over feeling something toward someone. Relationships were not my super-power, and I avoided them like the plague.

"Am I going to have to cuff you?" I tucked my thumbs into my service belt and stopped a few feet away from him.

He chuckled. "Is that what you're into, Sheriff?" His husky tone sent a shiver down my spine.

"Risky question." I took a few steps closer to where the dirt road gave way to open fields of tall grass that danced in the sudden breeze. "It could end well for you, or you could wind up in the drunk tank." I arched an eyebrow at him.

He turned to face me, his handsome features clothed in an inter-esting mix of low light and deep shadows.

"What makes you think one of those isn't ending well for me?" His devilish grin broke me, and I let out a laugh.

"I guess if that's what you like, I can oblige." I reached for my cuffs, and he lifted both hands in mock surrender. "But really, why are you out here?"

"Did Ethel call me in?" he asked, sounding unfazed.

I shifted my weight and scanned the field as the wind continued to toy with the dry grass. "Now isn't the time to be dodgy."

"Of course, she did." He let out a chuckle.

It didn't matter who had called him in; he was missing the point. "You're not supposed to be out here."

"I'm sorry, but it's a good place to think, and it's abandoned. I didn't mean any harm." He ran a hand through his dark hair, his body language still open and approachable despite the slight show of nerves.

The raw honesty of his words made me pause, and I swapped my sheriff's hat for my friend hat, the same way I would for anyone showing signs of distress. "What's on your mind?" I moved to stand shoulder to shoulder with him as he angled his body toward the old farmhouse. Under the moon's light, I saw the disrepair, the side panels falling away from the walls, the broken windows, the moss taking over an entire corner of the building.

"My dad built this place. It was his first real project. It was a passion project; off the books." His reflective tone drew the heart right out of my chest. "When I'm out here, I feel closer to him."

I nodded because there was nothing I needed to say. I'd stand there with Bayden for a few moments.

"But I'm ready to go," he mumbled with a sideways glance at me.

"I can give you a ride back." I lifted my shoulders, unsure if he was in any condition to drive.

He hesitated, then nodded. "That would be great. I'll have one of my brothers bring me back out tomorrow to get my truck."

"Noted," I said with a smile as we walked back toward my Tahoe.

On the way back, I took the surprise potholes more gently, though my water bottle still popped out of the holder. He caught the dark-blue bottle and tucked it back into its place.

"Thank you," I said.

He lifted a shoulder as if it was no big deal, but I hated the thing always escaping to crash around on the passenger floor. I'd been trying to fix it, but nothing had worked.

"Thank *you*," he said instead, staring out the window over the passing fields that enclosed the dirt road on both sides leading up to the old farmhouse. "For listening."

I sensed it was a struggle to open up and identified with that sentiment on more levels than I cared to admit. Sure, we talked, but it was never personal. Flirtatious? Yes. Intimate? No.

Before I could respond, he spoke up again. "And thanks, I guess, for not arresting me."

"You guess?" I said, arching an eyebrow at the road because there was no way I'd look at him.

"Well, there are worse things a beautiful woman could do to me, you know." I could imagine his panty-dropping smile, though I was immune—my panties weren't going anywhere.

If anyone else had said that, I'd be pissed. I'd feel like they were undermining my authority. But Bayden put me at ease, and our relaxed friendship had already proven he respected me far more than many people that blindly trusted me because of my badge. He didn't respect me out of obligation. He respected me because I'd proven I deserved his regard. There was a difference.

He angled his body toward me, tightening his belt as I pulled out onto the main highway. "Would you like to get a drink?" he asked in an even, hopeful tone.

I wanted to. I did. A beer sounded heavenly, but I shook my head no. "Can't, sorry. I'm on duty, and the city kind of frowns on officers drinking on the job."

"Where's your wild side—your sense of adventure?" He turned to stare at me. "Wait, the city only *kind of* frowns on it?"

He was something else.

I loved that he could make me laugh. I loved his quick humor and how easy he made our friendship. Despite the jokes and innuendo, which I was equally responsible for and an active participant most of the time, there were no expectations. There was no pressure. He was a friend, though the sexual attraction I had for him was anything but friendly.

Putting the brakes on those thoughts, I eased off the gas. No reason to speed on these roads in the dark. Not with the deer out and moving around under the light of the moon. Besides, I wasn't in a hurry since there wasn't much to do in a town with no actual crime.

"You're quiet tonight," he said.

I could feel his worried eyes studying me.

"It's Friday night, and I'm on a double shift." I usually worked twelve-hour shifts, but on Friday night, because of the occasional teen parties and minor issues like someone drinking too much and stumbling home, or even some random person trespassing at an old farmhouse, I worked a double.

"Need coffee?" He nodded at Roy's. Roy served coffee, but I wasn't sure I wanted to be seen in the bar.

"I can run in and grab you one to go if that helps."

On impulse, I pulled in, parked in a spot, and turned to him. "That sounds wonderful." I dug in my pocket, but he was out and gone before I could pull out my wallet. A few moments later, he was back with a steaming hot coffee in a cardboard to-go cup.

Bayden opened the door and got in. "Roy said he knows how you like it." He wiggled his eyebrows at me as the mouthwatering scent of —nonalcoholic—Irish cream and coffee met my nose.

"You're funny," I said, taking it and inhaling the steam before putting it in the cup holder on my side. I didn't like to put anything there because it was easy to bump with my knee, but I couldn't put it on his side where my water bottle was.

"Thanks."

I offered him money to pay for the coffee, and he stared at it, then at me as if I'd lost my mind. "I'm allowed to show my appreciation by buying an officer's coffee, right?"

I couldn't hold back a grin. "Thanks, but you don't have to do that."

"I know, but I want to." He buckled up, and I backed out and nosed the Tahoe toward his place with my heart feeling as warm as the coffee.

When I pulled in front of his house, I waited a second before speaking. "Try not to break the law, okay?"

He gave me a quick salute along with that cavalier grin that told me I hadn't seen the last of him before he climbed out of the SUV and headed toward his front door. I waited until he opened the door, worried about the melancholy attitude he had when I'd caught him at the old farm. He spun around in the doorway to face me with a warm smile on his face.

With a shake of my head, I pulled away from the curb. Bayden Lockhart was trouble, and I knew it.

CHAPTER TWO

BAYDEN

The sun hadn't quite dipped below the edge of the trees surrounding the old farm. With the gentle breeze, soft sunshine, and the aroma of sweet, warm grasses filling my lungs, it was as if I'd stepped back into my childhood.

I could still hear Dad's voice as he explained to me all the things we could build with our hands, but how anything we did, we needed to make sure we put our hearts into too.

With a slight smile, I thought about the real reason I'd come here tonight. Miranda was due to be off any time, and I tried to be her last call of the night. I drove slowly past Ethel and Norman's, so there was no way they would miss my dust plume on the road.

I reached out and ran my hand through the tall grass as the frogs began their evening serenade. This laid-back way wasn't how I expected to get her attention. I'd always been one to wear my heart on my sleeve, and I had a tendency to fall in love quickly, but there was something different with Miranda, and I didn't want to mess it up.

If that meant taking it slow, I'd crawl forward.

Miranda had turned down every date offer from day one, but

never in an *"I'm not interested"* way. More of an *"I can't because of insert reason here"* kind of way. Her concession on Friday night for coffee might have been a sign she wasn't putting me off. It wasn't exactly a date, but that small step felt like progress.

My phone dinged, and I pulled it out of my pocket. Quinn's text asked me where the hell I was and why I missed drinks? The "was" in his sentence meant they'd already left the bar.

That was better than I could have hoped for because I fully expected to bump into them if Miranda accepted my offer. It was Monday, and Quinn knew I'd been at work, so there was no reason to panic over my absence. I shoved my phone back into my pocket as the familiar sound of a Tahoe coming up the road filled my ears.

Little flocks of birds rose out of the grass to grab bugs right out of the sky. I whistled to them, and one trilled in response before Miranda exited her SUV and closed her door.

I couldn't see her expression with my back to her, but I could picture it in my mind's eye—slightly annoyed with her dark eyes narrowed. Her dusky rose lips would be tight as if holding back a smile—an arched eyebrow daring me to push my luck.

"Are you stalking me?" I threw the baiting words out there, and she rewarded me with a snort.

"The same way I stalk most criminals, yeah."

I winced. That one stung. "Let's keep the Taser above the belt, please." There was some entertainment in teasing her. Her humor lined right up with mine, and it was fun. Simple. Enjoyable.

"So, you like being cuffed and locked up, but not tased. I'll keep that in mind." Her throaty voice had every muscle in my core tightening up with lust. Damn, she could mess with me.

"What about you?" I asked as she stepped to my side, her gaze scanning the fields and watching the birds swoop and glide. "Do you like being cuffed, locked up, and tased?"

Her eyes met mine, though she didn't turn her head. "Wouldn't you like to know?"

Yes, yes, I would. That's why I asked. But I knew Miranda would not give me the satisfaction of knowing, and it didn't matter. Sex wasn't the goal with Miranda. I didn't want another notch in my bedpost. I wasn't sure exactly what I wanted, but it wasn't about sex, kinky or otherwise.

"You ready to cuff me, officer?" I offered her my wrists, still taunting her, even though I didn't want to find myself in cuffs. That was never the plan.

She sighed. "That's a lot of paperwork, and this is my last call of the day. So how about you run along and stop trespassing and working up poor Ethel?"

"Last call of the day?" I kept my tone perfectly neutral, though she knew right away that this was all going according to my plan. "Does that mean you're done working then?"

She nodded, her dark eyes locking on my face. A slight smile tugged the corners of her lips, and I wanted to lean in and kiss them. The breeze brought her perfume's scent to my nose—something light and citrusy that made my mouth water.

"Well, since I don't want to create more paperwork for you, I'll head on out, then." Jerking a thumb toward my truck, I flashed a grin, and a wary light flashed in her eyes. "I'm going to Roy's. I'd love to buy you a beer."

That eyebrow of hers twitched on its way to her hairline. "Are you trying to bribe an officer of the law?"

"Never. I offered to get out of here, so you don't have to arrest me, then told you where I was going and asked you to join me." Yeah, she was on to me. I could tell in the way her eyes studied my face.

Her lips parted, and I braced for her to call me out on what I'd done, but she didn't. Instead, she inhaled and exhaled, her shoulders lowering several inches as if that breath deflated her.

"Sure, but I need to go home, grab a quick shower, and change."

Her words hit me like a bolt of lightning. The thought of her in the shower nearly sank my battleship, and I gulped. This woman somehow had the power to revert me to the teenaged boy who couldn't go three seconds without thinking about sex. "Sounds great. Do you want me to follow you or meet you at Roy's?"

This time she didn't hold back the smile tugging the corners of her lips. With a tilt of her head and a side-eyed glance at me, she answered. "Don't push your luck. I'll meet you at Roy's."

"Whoa, you're reading too much into that. I wasn't suggesting anything but merely offering to come with you." Even though I'd offered to go back to her place—yes, with impure thoughts about her in the shower—I legitimately hadn't intended anything beyond accompanying her.

We walked back toward my truck and her SUV, and I watched her tuck her thumbs into her belt as she walked. She might be smaller than me, but there was a commanding presence to her I admired. Miranda took nothing from nobody.

"I'll be quick." She glanced up at me.

"I'll be waiting." With that, we separated into our vehicles, and she waved for me to pull out before her. I did; a slight smile on my face. We were going on a date—finally.

Careful to drive safely with her behind me, I monitored her in the rearview until we parted ways on the main road. She went toward home, and I headed toward Roy's. I must have sped the whole damn way because I was pulling into the parking lot moments later. I found an empty spot, sucked in a deep breath, and let it out. "Don't screw this up."

Miranda mattered. Any other woman and I wouldn't give a damn if they didn't like me. I wouldn't care if things didn't go well because if we weren't a good match, then so be it, but there was something between Miranda and me. Something I didn't want to destroy. Something that felt important, even if I couldn't explain it.

I got out of my truck and headed inside Roy's.

I breathed a sigh of relief that my brothers weren't there. Angie locked eyes with me, then made her way to where I was.

"Can I talk to you about—"

I lifted a hand to cut her off. "Look, you had an idea, we tried it, and it didn't work." I'd never actually been interested in her, but a deal's a deal, and I held up my end. It was not my fault she didn't get the outcome she wanted. If she wanted to play games, she had to be willing to lose. Maybe next time she'd just talk to the person she actually wanted to date. Anger lashed in her features, and she studied my face before spinning around and walking away.

I signaled Roy with two fingers, and he nodded, giving the empty spot next to me a significant glance. I shook my head a bit and glanced toward the door to show I'd have company shortly. One thing I'd always loved about Roy was how communicative he was without words.

It was a skill we'd discussed; it was easy to carry on an entire conversation without ever speaking a single word. Roy nodded and glanced at the clock before lifting an empty glass in my direction. I knew this was his way of telling me he'd bring our drinks when she showed up.

Angie settled down in a dark corner, her elbows on the table and her shoulders hunched forward protectively. For an instant, I felt terrible for her. Had I made the wrong call? Should I have done more to help her?

Then the voice of reason kicked in. If Angie wanted something, she needed to go for it, not ask me to play head games to help her get what she was looking for. I had my own life to live, and I had no plan to screw up my relationships for her.

The door opened, and I caught sight of Miranda. Her damp hair was free-flowing down to her waist instead of her usual no-nonsense bun. She still had that commanding set to her shoulders, even in plain clothes. Her fierce eyes met mine, and a smoldering smile played on her lips.

As Miranda made her way to me, I caught Angie's stare but ignored her. I patted the seat beside me, and Miranda slid onto it.

Almost instantly, Kandra materialized and put two beers in front of us.

"Hey, you two." Kandra smiled widely.

"How are you?" Miranda asked Kandra, and I watched the two talk while picking up my beer.

Kandra put a hand on her swollen belly and lifted a shoulder. "Tired. Good. Happy." I knew my sister-in-law was due any day, but she stubbornly refused to stop working, even though Noah offered her the option. She told us that working helped keep her mind off what could go wrong and focus on what was going right. She enjoyed being active, and we all respected that.

"You're looking beautiful." Miranda took a drink of her beer.

"I feel like a beached whale." Kandra laughed and hurried off to talk to someone signaling her, but not before giving me a significant glance. Damn. She was going to tell my brothers all about this date.

"I'm happy for her." Miranda turned to me, and I nodded.

"Kids are a game-changer." I'd never been sure about having kids of my own. While I loved family life, having someone wholly dependent on me was another thing. Frankly, the thought scared the hell out of me.

"Yeah." Miranda closed up like a flower at dusk, and I wondered what I'd said to upset her.

"Thank you for coming out with me. I know it's a big deal." As the sheriff, she had to protect her reputation. I understood that. The sheriff seeing someone would be news in our small town, and to my knowledge, she hadn't dated anyone since moving here. "Tell me about yourself."

She fiddled with her beer, then took a deep drink. "What's to know? I was in the Reserve. I was once a horseback riding champ. I took this job when it opened up."

"Reserve? National Guard?" I hadn't known specifics but assumed she was ex-military or something similar.

She nodded, her throat shifting as she swallowed hard and took another drink without meeting my gaze.

Before I could try to put her at ease, her phone rang.

She answered, and when the voice on the other end of the line spoke, all color drained from her face. Her eyes widened, and her hands trembled.

Her eyes flashed to me, and she held up a finger. "Yeah, I'm here." With that, she slid out of her seat and headed for the door, leaving me stunned and alone. In all the years I'd known her, I'd never seen her scared. But when I looked at her now, there was nothing but panic written all over her face.

CHAPTER THREE

MIRANDA

"I'll never forgive you." My mother's voice cut through me like an icy winter wind, and my knees nearly buckled as I made my way outside.

"I know." My throat screamed as if I'd swallowed a mouthful of crushed glass and chased it with an extra-tall unsweetened lemonade from a salt-rimmed glass. I pulled open the door and crawled into the back seat. Curling with my knees to my chest, I bit down on my lower lip as she continued to berate me.

"Everything that happened; it was your fault. All of it!" Mom's voice rose to a shrill screech, and I blinked back hot tears.

"Okay." There was nothing to say. Nothing I could say to defend myself. It wasn't my fault, but I'd grown used to my mother's accusations and knew better than to argue with her. Hidden behind the dark glass, I lifted and glanced at the door to Roy's, praying Bayden would respect my privacy. I couldn't face him. Not now. Not with my mother on the line.

Winding my arm around knees, I held the phone to my ear and waited for the rest of her razor-sharp words.

"Okay? None of this is okay!" She mocked my words before

sounding shocked at my answer. "You ran off to pretend you're some hero, but we remember. We remember who you are and what you did."

I flinched as if her words physically assaulted me and caused pain to flow through every pore in my body. "I'm sorry." And I was sorry. I was sorry she believed it was my fault. Sorry I couldn't face her, and even more sorry that we couldn't fix the rift between us.

"Oh, you're sorry." She must have moved the phone away from her mouth because her next words were muffled. "She says she's sorry," she shouted, probably at my dad. Her voice returned full force. "You're right. That brings your sister back. Sorry fixes everything."

My throat closed, and the scalding tears slipped down my cheeks. This time of year never got any easier.

"When are you coming home?" Her screech dug at the base of my skull like a dull ice pick, and I shuddered, swallowing back a wave of nausea.

"I'm not." I promised myself a long time ago that I'd never go back.

Her voice rose to a blood-curdling scream that reminded me of the time I'd happened across a raccoon with its paw stuck in a trap. "That's because you can't face what you've done."

She was right. I couldn't face the past. I did everything I could to run from it. I'd left home for the Guard, then wound up in Cross Creek. But no matter how far I ran, I couldn't escape what happened. No matter how hard she pushed, how much she blamed me, and how loud she yelled, it didn't make my sister's death my fault.

I wanted to tell her I needed to get off the phone, but I knew better. She'd keep calling back, nonstop, until she got it out of her system. There was no doubt she'd been drinking, and when she drank, she was impossible. Not that she was a peach when she was sober.

"How can you live with yourself?" Her voice rang in my ears as I glanced at the door and watched someone leave the bar. I only dared breathe when I saw it was Angie and not Bayden. She made her way to her beat-up Honda and slid into the driver's seat.

Angie didn't start the car, but sat there, hands on top of the wheel, staring into space. In the low light, I swear I saw the glitter of tears rolling down her cheeks.

"Why don't you just go be with her?" My mother's words hit my heart like a hollow point bullet, penetrating, then shredding everything in my chest. "Why don't you just go be with her? You couldn't even protect her, so what makes you think you deserve to be here?"

My shoulders slumped, and I curled tighter into myself. Struggling to breathe around my agony, I glanced at Angie once again. She'd tilted her head back on the headrest and stared at the roof of her car. Her chest rose and fell as if she were taking deep breaths. I followed suit even as my mother lowered her voice to a broken whisper to deliver a final blow.

"It should have been you instead of her."

Angie turned over her little car's engine and pulled out of the lot as the line went dead. Mom had hung up, finally. Dropping my phone onto the seat beside me, I hugged myself as pain washed over me in waves.

On some level, there was truth to her accusations. I hadn't protected my sister when she needed me most. I hadn't saved her.

With a deep, shaking breath, I blinked back the tears and swallowed all the emotions eating me alive. The joy of the night and casual fun with Bayden seemed so far away now.

Sunk in a bottomless pit of despair, I stared through the metal squares separating the Tahoe's front and back seats. I reached out with one hand, pressing my fingers through the metal grate and clinging to it like a child gripping a chain-link fence.

I only ever wanted to help others who found themselves powerless, in pain, trapped, stuck, or struggling with demons. That was why I became a soldier and why I'm a sheriff. My time as an upholder of the law taught me that most problems aren't solved with cuffs or jail time. Sure, those things had their place, but it was kindness that people needed most. It could come in any form from a smile, a ride, or a warning rather than a ticket.

My phone dinged, and I picked it up, steeling myself and fighting back panic. Bayden's text knotted the muscles in my neck and shoulders, and a stabbing pain flashed behind my right eye.

Are you okay?

No. No, I wasn't okay.

Before he could come looking for me, I exited the back seat and climbed behind the wheel. Closing the door behind me, I turned the key and listened to the engine roar to life.

My only thought was about going home and finding safety in my little bungalow. As I pulled out of the parking lot, the door opened, and Bayden's silhouette filled the space as the light from the inside escaped around him.

Fresh tears flowed down my cheeks as I drove away. Bayden deserved better than the lousy company I'd be tonight.

Driving like the devil was on my tail, I sped home, pawing at the never-ending tears that continued to fall. When I pulled into my driveway, I opened the garage door and parked inside. Rushing for the door, I let myself in and breathed as if this was the first oxygenated air I'd encountered all day. Tears continued to seep down my face while I pulled off my jacket and rushed for the bathroom.

Turning on the cold water in the shower, I undressed and stepped inside. Hunkering down, I curled into a tight ball with my legs folded to my chest and tucked my forehead against my knees. Icy water coated my flesh. I rocked back and forth, letting myself go numb until all of it felt like a bad dream.

My phone rang from my pants pocket on the floor, but I ignored it. I couldn't face anyone.

Not my mother.

Not Bayden.

Not anyone.

Not right now.

As a shiver started deep within my bones, I focused on slowing my breath. I stared at the white tiles under my feet, clearing my mind of all but three thoughts that refused to leave me alone. Like angry hornets, they buzzed furiously around my head.

I became a sheriff to help people.

But I couldn't help the person closest to me—my sister.

In truth, I couldn't help myself.

What good was I?

When I finally stood, my vision went white, and I clutched the shower door with one hand and pressed the other flat to the tile wall.

A heartbeat passed, and I wondered if this was it. Would my deputy find me dead? Surely they'd come looking for me if I didn't show up for work. They'd likely find my naked body and think I'd fallen in the shower, but the truth was I'd died of a broken heart.

My vision cleared, and I breathed out as the trembling deep in my body continued. Turning the water off, I grabbed my towel and wrapped it around me. What I needed was to climb into bed. I could deal with everything else tomorrow—everything except one thing.

I left Bayden so suddenly that I knew he'd worry, and I needed to let him know what was going on. There was no way I could tell him the truth because I told no one my darkest secrets. I didn't share much about myself. It was safer that way.

I'd tell him I had a headache and had come home to go to bed.

As that stabbing sensation behind my right eye flared up again, I took comfort that my excuse wasn't precisely a lie.

Just then, my phone rang, and I fished it out of my pants pocket with hands that felt more like flippers. None of my fingers wanted to work. They were numb and unresponsive, but I answered Bayden's call.

"Hello."

"Are you okay?" The concern in his voice tore at me, and I struggled to keep my tone casual.

"Yeah, sorry. The headache came on suddenly. I'm going to go to bed. Can I have a rain check on beers?" I absentmindedly rubbed the back of my neck.

"Sure, no problem." The worry still crept into his words, and I wanted to comfort him and not draw attention to his concern, but I refused to face this head-on.

Not with him.

Not with anyone.

Not with myself.

"Thank you. I'm looking forward to it." Even as I said the words, I realized they were hollow. This time of year was always challenging, and I knew that enjoying myself would be impossible for weeks until things passed, the calls stopped, and the memories faded.

Family was paramount to the Lockharts. Growing up with parents who made you feel like you were never good enough, made adult relationships seem impossible.

Goose bumps broke out on my skin, and sweat beaded across my brow as my hands shook.

"Same." He didn't sound convinced, but I lacked the ability or desire to keep talking. As if reading my mind, he spoke again. "I hope you feel better soon. Headaches are the worst."

I nodded, fully aware he couldn't see me even as another bolt of pain stabbed through my brain. "I'm going to get some rest. Thank you again for tonight, and sorry to be such a party pooper." *Party pooper?* What was I, a sixty-year-old woman? I'd never used that term before in my life.

He didn't seem to notice. "Don't worry about it. I want you to feel better. Take care of yourself, and let me know if there's anything you need, okay?"

I nodded again, like an idiot. "Okay. I'll do that." He was so sweet. I didn't doubt he knew there was more meaning in my silence than my words.

"Have a good night."

"You too." We hung up, and I stared at the phone, aware that I'd had the worst call and best call of the month in one night.

Life was crazy.

I liked Bayden, really liked him. But I didn't see how we could make it work. The things we needed and wanted were too different.

That reality meant we could never be together, and, if possible, that left me even more grief-stricken than before.

CHAPTER FOUR

BAYDEN

Everything about how we'd left that last interaction Monday night bothered me. Miranda had taken a call that had been clearly distressing. Then she bailed on our date without saying a word. She hadn't responded to my first couple of texts, and when she finally answered the phone, things seemed ... off.

I worried about her. As I pulled into her driveway Wednesday afternoon, I tried to think of what I was going to say. How did I tell her I was concerned without coming across as creepy or overprotective? I knew she could handle herself. Hell, other than my mom, she was likely the strongest woman I knew.

I didn't need to screw this up. Whatever Miranda was going through, she didn't trust me enough to confide in me, yet. That was her right, but I wanted her to know I was there for her in any capacity she needed.

I killed the engine and got out of my truck, walking up to her front door like I belonged. The doorbell trilled, and I hoped she wasn't out or busy. As close as we'd gotten, she didn't share details of her life with me. I didn't know what her hobbies were, or what she liked to do for fun, or even what she did on her days off.

Maybe she was at the creek swimming, or she went out of town to see family. Hell, she could have even driven to the city to go to the mall.

The last one didn't seem like her, but she didn't share much about herself with me, so it was possible.

The door opened, quelling my doubts about her whereabouts instantly. Dark circles under her eyes led me to believe she hadn't slept well, and her pinched expression told me she wasn't happy to have me on her doorstep.

"What are you doing here?" She crossed her arms, blocking the opening in the doorway as if to keep me out.

And all the plans I'd had for what to say flew out of my brain. I hadn't expected Miranda not to want to see me. To be honest, the rejection stung. "I was hoping we could talk about what happened the other night. Like adults." The second I said the words, I wished I could yank them back.

Her eyes narrowed, and she lifted on the balls of her feet like a boxer ready to throw a mean right hook. She jabbed instead. "Adults usually call first. They don't just show up."

I let out a sigh and tried to decompress. "I'm sorry. It's just ... this," I gestured between us to indicate the budding relationship we were cultivating, "is important to me."

She relaxed a little, but only slightly. Her shoulders dropped an inch, and her weight shifted back to her heels before leveling out. That tiny gesture gave me the confidence to press forward and reveal more of the truth. Maybe it was stupid to put myself out there, but I had to try something because what I was doing wasn't working.

"I'd like to be here for you when you need someone." *I sound like an idiot.*

She tensed up again, and I wanted to groan. Why was I here again? She didn't want me here. But I continued talking because I'd left my common sense in the truck. "If you want that too, let me in."

She shifted to the right, bumping the door. It squeaked open another inch, and I opened my mouth again.

"Not literally. You know what I mean." My attempt at light-hearted humor fell flat, and I wanted to fix it but didn't know how.

She blinked, then closed up again. "See, that's where you're wrong, Bayden." Her calm tone reminded me of that silent, electrifying hum before lightning strikes. "I don't have to do anything. I owe you nothing."

"You're right, you don't owe me anything. But an explanation would be nice," I said, frustrated. What in the hell happened? She'd never been like this before. She'd never pushed me away like this either. Had I done something to upset her? Other than showing up unannounced? But something told me that this wasn't because of me. I was on the receiving end of something else that was bothering her.

Her eyes widened at my words, but she seemed to have nothing to say.

That was fine with me; I had plenty left to say. "We went out for drinks, you took a phone call, ran out on me, left without a word, didn't answer my texts, then an hour later answered my call to tell me you had a headache. You scared the hell out of me!" As my stress bubbled over, I shoved a hand through my hair, hating that my fingers were shaking. This was so important to me, but it wasn't going well at all.

"That's not my problem! Maybe you scare too easily." Her arms tightened across her chest like she was protecting herself from me, and I backed up a half step. The white of her knuckles and the way her fingers dug into her arm confused me. She seemed pissed. I wanted to know why, but I doubted she was in the mood to answer my questions.

"Then, I show up here to make sure you're okay and to talk about it like a damn adult, and you tell me you don't owe me anything." Why didn't she understand what I was trying to say?

Her voice rose. "I don't!"

How could I explain myself better? I took a deep breath to calm down and responded. "I never said you did. I said that this is important to me. You're important to me. I never said you owe me anything."

Her eyes lit up with an almost feverish glitter that surprised me. "Why? Why am I important to you, Bayden? What do you know about me? What reason could you possibly care this much about a near stranger?"

She took a step toward me, her arms dropping to her sides and her fists balling up. As she leaned forward, I backed up another step.

But she wasn't finished talking. "You're building the new station. Thank you. I'm sorry if I led you to believe there's more to this than that." As she said the words, tears filled her eyes, and her voice broke. And I knew she wasn't honest. "We're working together. That's it."

"Then why agree to drinks?"

She seemed flustered. "Co-workers drink together."

"So do friends, and I'm your friend, Miranda." Why was she doing this? "I know you were in the Guard. I know you hate pickles; it's blasphemy. You think fruit shouldn't be on pizza, which makes tomatoes feel awkward. I know you love beer, that you're good at your job, and you don't think locking everyone up is the answer. You're a good person." As I spoke, she seemed to relax again.

"Look, I know something is up with you. I get it. Sometimes life sucks, but I'm here when you're ready to talk because that's what friends do."

But she shook her head. I wasn't sure what she was saying no to, but the universal gesture was unmistakable.

"Do you want me to go?" I asked, taking another step back, "because I'll go. I didn't come here to upset you. I hope you know that."

The tears sparkling in her eyes made me ache for her, but she didn't say a word. She seemed frozen in place, her face begging me to stay, but her body language demanding I go.

"I won't give up on you because you had a bad day. Everybody has bad days, and bad things happen." I spread my arms, wanting more than anything for her to step into them for a hug. But she didn't.

"Just go," she whispered as if she couldn't trust her voice.

I studied her, unsure. Then—without another word—I turned and walked back to my truck.

Behind the wheel, I backed out and drove aimlessly. As I went through town, I wished I could call my dad for advice. I'd give anything to hear his voice and listen to his words of wisdom regarding women.

I parked at Roy's and headed inside. Finding a dark corner, I sat down and ordered a beer. Kandra was off, and Roy brought me the brew, hesitated, then sat down across from me.

"What happened?"

I glanced at him, surprised.

He let out a chuckle. "Son, I know women problems when I see them." With a glance around, he leaned in and spoke in a lower voice. "I might not seem like it, but I'm not terrible with women."

"Don't let him lie to you," Gypsy said from a few tables away. "He's terrible. Clueless, really. He hasn't even asked me out yet." She continued to eat her garlic knots, her brows high and incredulous.

"I'll get to it when I'm ready!" He turned away from her and hunched his shoulders. "See? Can't even keep 'em away."

I chuckled. It had never even occurred to me that those two might consider getting together. Roy lost his wife nearly a decade before, and Gypsy had long since divorced her ex-husband. It was a step up for her, by all accounts, and I was happy she was getting away from a garbage guy. She was a sweet woman that deserved someone good.

"I heard that!"

He winced slightly at her words, and I couldn't hold back my smile.

"I screwed up. But I'm not sure how." I didn't even know where to start. Everything was so damn complicated.

"Well, I'm not the type to gossip, but I know that a certain sheriff has her demons. I'd say, be patient and kind and there when she needs you." Roy's congenial tone helped put me at ease. He was telling me to do exactly what I'd been doing and what I planned to keep doing.

"Thank you."

"The quiet ones are always trouble." Gypsy laughed. "They're tougher nuts to crack, but well worth it."

"I think you're the only nut here," Roy said over his shoulder, "and you've already cracked!"

Gypsy nodded her head. "True, true." She adjusted the strap of her tie-dyed dress and smoothed her hair back into her bun.

"And if you screwed up, give her some space, then apologize. Let her cool off, then dust off and get back in the ring." He lifted both shoulders. "Unless she's told you flat out she's not interested, then step back until she comes to you. If she doesn't, she's not the one for you."

"You make it sound so easy." I took a deep gulp of my beer.

"Because it is. It only seems tough because you're living it. You're in your head, making everything more difficult." Roy shifted in his seat as if expecting Gypsy to chime in. But she didn't.

"You're probably right."

He snorted. "Probably?"

"No, he's right. This time." Gypsy lifted both shoulders. "I mean, it worked with Noah and Kandra. I told him almost the same thing and look how that turned out."

"You got the two to talk again," Roy said to her, and she nodded. "Doesn't make you an expert."

"More of an expert than you. Who have you gotten back together?" She laughed at him, and he glared playfully at her.

"Well, I'm trying to work on this one, no thanks to you." He gestured at me as they talked, like I wasn't even there. And I chuckled, amused by them as I drank my beer. Yep, they sounded like a perfect couple.

"It is excellent advice," I told him. "We'll see how it works out for me soon enough." For some reason, I enjoyed the thought of those two making a competition out of playing matchmaker.

CHAPTER FIVE

MIRANDA

The weight of everything seemed heavier today than most days. I parked the Tahoe facing the main strip and sat for a few moments, composing myself. Taking a few deep breaths, I blew them out slowly and tried to shake the stress out of my hands. It didn't work. After the talk with my mother, I thought I was as low as I could get, and my life couldn't get any worse—I was wrong.

Now the look in Bayden's eyes as he said, *I won't give up on you because you had a bad day* haunted me. But I felt worse when I thought about the look in his eyes when I'd told him to go. I couldn't get the defeated set to his shoulders when he'd walked away out of my mind's eye. I couldn't stop thinking about how hurt he'd been.

My hands tightened around the wheel, and my knuckles went white. The leather squeaked under the pressure of my grip, but I didn't ease up.

I hurt him, and all he'd wanted to do was help me.

I didn't want to push him away, but I didn't know what else to do. We couldn't be together because it wouldn't work. I was broken. My parents tore me down every chance they could. I didn't know what a loving relationship looked like or how to be in one.

It didn't matter that I wanted to be with him because we weren't right for each other. Maybe I wasn't a suitable match for anyone.

My hands ached, and I let go of the wheel and sat watching the traffic. The day had been quiet, as usual, but I would not complain about that. I wasn't sure I could handle anything too serious. I'd been ready to call in my deputy if I wound up in something over my head, but thankfully, I hadn't had to.

My mind kept drifting back to Bayden. What else could I do? I mean, a clean break seemed kinder. Now all I had to do was avoid him until he got married or one of us died of old age. That wouldn't be too hard because he was good-looking— if I was honest, hot is more like it. Some woman would snatch him right up. And if he decided to be a stubborn ass and never marry, well, one of us eventually had to die.

I would have laughed if the thought wasn't so damn depressing.

Patti came out of her shop and gave me a little wave.

I stepped out of the Tahoe and walked toward her. She smiled, her hazel eyes looking almost honey-colored in the sunshine. The sun picked out red highlights from her tawny-colored hair, and she waited for me to approach.

"You know, I'd love to see you in yellow. Like a sundress." She pulled me in for a hug, and I tried to smile. "How's life?"

"It goes. How are you?" I pulled back and studied her as she stood outside her shop and stretched a bit, waving at someone as they drove past.

"Good, good. And how is Bayden?" She was staring at me like she could read my mind if she focused on my expression hard enough.

I gave a slight shake of my head, lifted my shoulders, and spread my hands. "Fine, I guess. I'm not sure."

Her expression dropped a bit. "Oh. I thought you two were dating now. That's a shame."

"Oh, no. We're not dating." I let out a chuckle and stood my ground as she danced around me. Patti was another person who always knew what was happening. She knew who was looking for love, who was single, and who was the perfect match for everyone else.

"Need a trim?" she asked me, nudging her head toward her salon. "It's on the house. I'm not busy today."

I shook my head. "Can't. If something were to happen while I was in your chair, well, you know ... but I'm happy to stay and visit for a few."

She didn't seem to like my answer.

"Thank you for the offer though," I said, and she lit up.

"You're very welcome. You're fabulous at your job, you know. I'm glad you're the sheriff." Her thoughtful eyes traced my face, then left to watch the traffic.

"Thank you. I'm proud to be here." It was hard to carry on a simple conversation with Bayden running circles through my mind.

She smiled at me. "You know, Bayden's a good guy too. I'd been hoping he'd find the perfect woman to settle down with."

She wasn't subtle. I'd give her that. I wasn't sure what to say, and I didn't like being on the spot when I already felt off balance. "He is a good man, and I also hope he finds the right woman." With a smile frozen on my face, I tried to figure out how to back out of the conversation gracefully. The thought of Bayden with another woman left a bitter taste in my mouth, which made little sense. He had every right to see whomever he wanted, so why did that bother me? I was the one turning him down and pushing him away, not the other way around.

"You know," she said, giving me a sideways glance as she danced a step closer to me on the light-gray concrete sidewalk outside her salon, "some people think you're the woman for him."

I chuckled. "Honey, I'm so busy I don't have time to think about men. It wouldn't be fair for him to have to put up with my hectic schedule."

She snorted. "Oh, please. Plenty of sheriffs have families and even kids."

I froze.

"He'd be lucky to have you." She smiled at me, and I struggled to respond.

"Maybe I'd be the lucky one." I choked the words out but somehow sounded smooth and conversational. It wasn't possible. Patti didn't know it, the town didn't know it, Bayden didn't know it, but things would never work between us. No matter how badly anyone wanted it to happen.

She laughed. "Oh, you're so sweet, and I love that."

I wished I could feel half as lighthearted as she seemed. As the world crushed down on my shoulders, the struggle between what I wanted and the right thing to do became painful. I had to remind myself that it didn't matter what everyone else thought—they didn't know the complete story.

"I'm sorry I'm such a meddler. I don't mean any harm." She seemed to grow serious for a moment.

I didn't mean to upset her or make her feel bad for trying to set us up. "I know, and it's sweet! Bayden is a great man."

"How about you?" I asked, and her attention jumped to me again. Her feet shuffled on the pavement, and she shifted her weight to the side. A slight breeze ruffled her free-flowing navy shirt, and her dangling silver earrings swayed a bit as she turned her head.

She was a handsome woman, and I didn't know how or why she was single.

"How about me? Are you trying to set me up with Bayden?" she snorted. "He's too young for me, love."

I shook my head. "No, I mean, is there a special man in your life? Met anyone promising?"

She paused, and I wondered if anyone ever asked her about herself. I knew she was busy, that she prided herself on knowing everything about everyone, but what about her? Maybe listening to her tell me more about herself would force Bayden from my thoughts. I'd be grateful for any reprieve from his hurt eyes and wounded walk as he left my step for his truck.

"I ... No." She paused and let out a sigh. I sensed her guard drop at the same time and focused wholly on her. "I'm happy helping people, you know?" she lifted her shoulders. "I love my job and this town, but it can be lonely if I'm honest."

I nodded. I understood loneliness all too well.

"I'm not getting any younger, but I am worried that I might never meet the right guy." Her hazel eyes traced the sun as it sank ever closer to the mountains.

I thought about it a moment. "Have you considered online dating?"

She glanced at me, and I hustled to explain.

"It's not as dangerous as it used to be. I can give you some information to help keep you safe. But there's not an endless pool of bachelors here, so meeting someone outside Cross Creek might be what you need." I flashed a smile as her expression shifted to one of stunned amazement. Her mouth went slack, and her eyes widened.

"I never even thought about online dating," she said.

I leaned in, and stage whispered, "You can do it on your phone." It was amazing to me that such a simple solution had never occurred to her. I was glad to assist her for once. I knew Patti did her best to help everyone and anyone. I mean, it wasn't even the first time she'd offered me a free haircut. It was a long-standing offer. She never charged me, but I always tipped her well. Patti did a fantastic job.

"Thank you!" She said, leaning in and hugging me.

"Let me get you that info before you start, okay? I want you to be safe." I caught her eyes, and she nodded.

"Now, why didn't I think of that?" She still seemed stunned.

I shrugged. "Sometimes, when we're close to something, it's easy to overlook." As I said the words, I thought about Bayden again. If only there were a simple solution for us. Not that online dating was always a piece of cake, because obviously, it had its unique challenges, but it wasn't impossible like Bayden and I were.

"I hope I didn't upset you by pushing you so hard." She studied my face, and I smiled.

"No worries. I'm not upset." And I wasn't. I knew she meant

well. Heck, I agreed with her. If I didn't know better, I'd think Bayden and I were a good fit too.

"Thank you for helping me." She lowered her voice as if she was about to reveal a secret. "I have been worried that I'd never meet someone. Nobody wants to grow old alone, right?"

Her words landed like a sucker punch to my gut, and the air whooshed out of my lungs. I didn't want to grow old alone, but what choice did I have? I pretended her words didn't affect me and smiled while answering. "Right."

My walkie keyed up. "Miranda?"

I lifted it and pressed the button. "Here," I said, taking a few steps away from Patti.

"We have a report of a suspicious vehicle out on Creekside Road."

Damn it, Bayden.

CHAPTER SIX

BAYDEN

Saturday had dawned bright and warm, so I decided it was now or never. I'd make my move, and she'd either shoot me down, or we'd wind up enjoying quality time together.

I regretted how our last conversation had gone, and I wasn't sure how to fix things. I planned an apology and something special. I would do my best to show Miranda I was serious.

The sound of her tires on the dirt warned me she was on her way up the drive, and I calmly watched her come into view. She parked, waited a few moments, then got out. The annoyance on her face told me a lot about her state of mind, and I reminded myself to be patient.

She slammed the SUV door and made her way toward me with an assured stride that was as no-nonsense as I've ever seen. She spoke quickly with her thumbs tucked into her belt and a strange refusal to meet my gaze while scanning the fields. The sun was finally settling down over the mountain ridges, and the glow from my truck grew more pronounced with every passing moment.

"What the hell are you doing, Bayden?"

I glanced at my truck; I was pretty sure it was obvious what I was doing. Refusing to be thrown by Miranda's clipped tone and frosty greeting, I headed for the back of my truck. "Well, I figured you could use a break. You have your walkie, and this is a great chance to unwind. Plus, if I'm not mistaken, you're at the end of your shift, so..." I glanced at her as I lowered the tailgate.

I'd strung little, fat round bulbs along the truck's bed for light. In the bed was an air mattress that I'd already inflated and covered in fresh sheets and blankets. I placed a stocked cooler in the back seat of my king cab. We could reach through the open back window and grab a beer or snacks.

It was a date night setup and perfect for the two of us to enjoy our privacy. I wanted to spend some quality time with her, and given how our last attempt at a date had turned out, I decided it was time to try a different tactic.

"No, I mean, what the hell are you doing?" Exhaustion wrapped around her words like a wet blanket, and I struggled to keep my enthusiasm. Damn, I was striking out left and right with this woman.

"Well, since our last date ended in disaster." I met her gaze finally, but hers skipped away. "I tried something different." With a slight smile, I ran my hand through my hair. Was she going to tell me off? She looked like she wanted to tell me off. But as I watched, she inhaled as if to speak, but held the breath a moment, then slowly deflated.

"You're cute, you know that?" Her tone wasn't exactly friendly, but my smile stretched across my face.

"Thanks. Right back at ya." Was I mistaken? Was that a positive response? She leaned away from me; her expression suddenly troubled. "Look, I'm sorry for upsetting you when I showed up at your place. That wasn't my intention. I just wanted to make sure you were okay."

She gave a slight nod. "I know. And I'm sorry for popping off at you." Her tired eyes met mine, then left again, and I sensed there was more she wanted to say. "This is sweet." She nodded at the back of my truck.

"What you can't see is the cooler in the back seat. It's loaded with beers and snacks." I let out a slight chuckle, and a smile slowly spread across her lips. "What do you say? Are we going to give this dating thing another go?"

The struggle in her body language was clear. She leaned toward her vehicle as if internally telling herself she should go, but something seemed to pull her back in my direction as if she wanted to stay. Her features tightened as if the walls had come up. She didn't want to share this fight with me.

"No pressure. If you want to leave, I'll go first so you can make sure the hoodlum is off the property and your job is done." I offered a grin and shoved my hands deep in my pockets. She always had me feeling like a damn teenager.

She lifted her shoulders, then headed back to her Tahoe. My heart dropped, and I waited; she was going to leave. A few moments passed, and the engine didn't start. I headed to my truck and grabbed my water bottle to give her more time to decide, but inside I was at war. If this didn't work, how would I come back swinging? Was she interested or not? Had I been reading her all wrong since the beginning?

Her door closed—much less forcefully this time—and I glanced in her direction. She'd taken off her belt and jacket. The white tank top was much more relaxed, and she arched a challenging eyebrow at me as if daring me to say something.

"I'm off duty," she said with a slight lift of one shoulder.

My abs tightened, but I internally cautioned myself that she might not be staying.

"What now?" she asked, studying my face.

I nodded to the back of the truck, my hopes rising another notch. "We climb in and talk and laugh and eat snacks and drink beer."

Her lips twitched. "I've never been on a date like this."
Neither had I.
Her voice softened. "I've never been with a guy like you."
I could only hope that was a good thing. "Little secret?" I asked,

leaning in as if to tell her some juicy gossip. "I've never been with a guy like me either."

She chuckled at my nervous joke. I gave her a hand into the truck and climbed in behind her. As she settled onto the bed, her fingertips traced one of the fat bulbs. "This is great, you know." She glanced at me as I settled in next to her.

"Thanks. Want a beer?" I reached in and offered her a cold one. She took it, and I grabbed mine. Together, we popped the tops and clanked our bottles before we let the refreshing amber liquid quench our thirsts. "How was your day?" I asked, hoping my cheesy question would elicit another laugh from her.

"Actually, it was strange. Patti tried to set you and me up, and I helped her get into online dating." She laughed and gave a little head shake as if the world was going to hell.

"Maybe the universe is trying to tell you something." I took a drink of my beer and offered her a smile.

She lifted her beer with a slight shrug. "Maybe."

"Tell me more about yourself." I wanted to know what made her tick. I wanted to know what made her who she was and everything she was willing to share. But at my question, she tensed up.

Her voice lowered. "I was an average kid, loved horses, and grew up in a home with both parents." She swallowed hard. "I was all around pretty normal."

"Were you an only child?"

She didn't answer. Instead, she took another drink and stared off into space. A minute passed, and then two. She spoke while staring at her bottle and scrubbing the corner of the label with her thumb. "What was it like, growing up with three brothers?"

I grinned. "Loud. Chaotic. Busy. Still is." I loved my brothers, even though they drove me nuts most days.

She smiled, but it looked more like a sad expression that tugged at something deep inside me.

"What brought you to Cross Creek?" Maybe pushing was a bad

idea, but I was interested in her. In her life, her past, everything about her.

Her eyes ticked to mine. "The chance to start over."

That heavy answer told me it was time to change the subject, but I couldn't help but try to lighten the moment. "Why? Are you secretly a bank robber?"

The corners of her lips lifted, and she shook her head.

I leaned in a little closer. "No, you're a gunslinger. The scariest, and I bet there's still a 'wanted ... dead or alive' poster out there with your picture on it."

She laughed. "How old do you think I am?"

"You're right. It can't be that. Maybe you're a child star who grew up and hid out in a small town hoping to stay unrecognized and live a private life." I leaned in a few more inches, and she lifted her hands, beer carefully held in one.

"You got me."

"I hope so," I said. Because every moment together was so comfortable and natural, I didn't want to let that feeling go. She wasn't throwing our fight back in my face like other women would have done in the past. We weren't holding grudges; we were communicating, having fun, and enjoying each other.

Her breath caught, and the hollow of her throat bottomed out as her gaze ticked back and forth between mine. I could smell the beer on her breath and the soft citrusy smell of her perfume. That combination of grapefruit and something else made my mouth water, and I wanted to taste her.

I knew she wasn't telling me everything. Maybe she didn't want to tell me everything about herself. That was fine; she didn't owe me anything. If and when she decided she wanted to talk to me about her life and past, I'd be here. But I'd wait until she was ready. I might pry a bit, but never enough that would make her uncomfortable.

Something ignited in her eyes as her gaze lowered to my lips. Her tongue traced her lower lip and left a slight sheen behind that made me desperately want her. "Can I kiss you, officer?" I asked, somewhat teasing, partially asking permission, and absolutely wanting to press my lips to hers.

Her eyes drifted across my face as if she were buying time to answer. "I'm off duty; it's Miranda right now." A slight glimmer of humor sparked in her eyes, and I knew she was leaving me hanging for giggles.

"Can I kiss you, *Miranda*?" The joke was on her. I could see the craving in her eyes, the heat, the passion, and knew this was as much torture for her as it was for me.

With a slight growl-like sound deep in her throat, she leaned in and kissed me. Her lips, warm and soft, and faintly beer-flavored, packed more of a punch than any fight I'd ever been in. She parted for me, inviting me in, and my tongue met hers. The silken slide woke a slumbering hunger in me, and I leaned into her. Her arm slipped around my shoulder, and she pulled me closer as the kiss deepened. As the sun sank out of sight and night sounds met my ears, I got lost in her.

She broke the kiss, then planted a chaste peck on my lips.

I kissed her again, then pulled back a little.

With a slight smile, she took another drink of her beer. I followed suit. A moment later, she leaned into me again. "I like kissing you," she whispered.

"I like kissing you too," I shot right back. Our lips met again, and that same heat blazed to life inside me. I was right; there was something different about Miranda. Because no other kiss had felt like this before, and I couldn't get enough of her. I knew then that I would break down every wall to get to her and to keep her safe from whatever was holding her back.

CHAPTER SEVEN

MIRANDA

It was stupid of me to let my guard down with Bayden last night. I awoke Sunday morning with nightmares that I didn't want to think too much about, so I let my thoughts shift to the previous night as I dragged myself into the shower.

He'd asked some questions I couldn't answer. But when I didn't answer, he didn't push. Instead, he left me with the feeling that not only could I tell him anything, but that he'd be ready to listen when I came to him. That made me somewhat hopeful, but even more terrified.

Cold water hit me square in the face before turning warm, and I stood there in shock for a moment as memories crashed back through my brain. *The water was so cold...*

Shaking my head, I forced my attention back to Bayden. Back to our date, our time together, and the sweet gestures he'd shown me. The date idea was the sweetest thing anybody had ever done for me. Talking with him was less stressful than I'd imagined or expected. And his kisses...

Heat flowed through my veins as I remembered his sky-blue eyes while he asked my permission to kiss me. There'd been something gentle, but something hungry in him. I sensed his control and respected that he didn't take what he wanted. I knew Bayden enough to see that he'd never get deterred, even when there were roadblocks, so I fully expected him to go for it and ravage me.

He'd surprised me.

I scrubbed my hair, trying to keep those other evil thoughts from creeping in; they had a way of nagging at the edges of my mind like demons waiting for the cover of darkness.

Although time with Bayden was enjoyable, I knew better than to get into a personal relationship because of all the things that haunt me. Besides that, I also needed to set a good example, and I let him sweep me up into breaking the law. Last night we were trespassing, and I let it go when it is my duty to do the right thing.

Despite the fact that everything inside me was telling me to stay away, part of me still hoped I'd bump into him again, or that he'd set me up like he had last night. There was something so fun and unexpected about that date that I was still replaying it in my mind. Nobody had ever done anything like that before. He'd considered everything and turned the night into something special, even though we didn't do more than kiss and drink a beer before deciding to turn in for the night. Partially because it got chilly quickly, and also there were the mosquitoes, but mostly it was because I got drowsy.

He'd driven behind me to be sure I got home safely, and that tiny gesture meant so much. He'd waited until I got inside and turned on my lights, then his truck pulled out and drove off. When he got home, he sent a text to let me know he was home safe too.

I readied myself for bed with a warmth in my chest and a newfound respect for him, and then I fell asleep quicker than I could remember in a long time.

But the nightmares...

Since sleep eluded me, I jumped in the shower. As I rinsed the soap from my hair and skin, I counted the tiles on the wall. Focusing on anything else helped. I wouldn't let my past drag down my day. "I don't live there anymore," I whispered to the empty room.

Feeling foolish, I turned off the water and grabbed my towel. An overwhelming sense of dread swept through me, and I shivered. The chill in the air attacked my warm skin as things struggled to surface.

I forced those uneasy feelings back and doubled down my focus on Bayden.

He'd told me he wanted to see me again.

I wanted to see him again too, but I knew it wasn't a good idea.

Dragging him into my life, into the middle of my unsolved problems ... it would be cruel. I could never be the woman he wanted, the woman he needed, and I had to be careful until he knew the truth. I didn't want to hurt him, and I didn't want to wind up hurt, so distance seemed to be the best option. *But was that possible?* Fully dressed and geared up, I lifted my head as the doorbell rang. Panic kicked in, and my heart galloped a steady beat as I stared at the front door.

"Miss Miranda," Max, our beloved and wise mailman's voice rang out, and all my fears dissolved.

With a few quick steps, I made my way to the door, slid the three deadbolts free, and pulled the door open. "Max," I said with a smile, genuinely glad to see him. "Good morning."

He offered me a box, and I took it with thanks. "Come on in," I said, swinging the door wide and taking the package into my kitchen table. "How are you today?" I asked. The smell of coffee made my mouth water as I set the package down.

"Doing well. But something tells me you're having a rough go of it this morning." His gentle tone didn't hide the worry in his voice.

I turned to face him, noting the seriousness in his eyes. I already knew Max's sixth sense was always in overdrive. The man could be a detective if he wished. He was a pro at ferreting out the truth and seeing through the facades people put up.

I sighed. "You're right. It's been a rough morning." There was no use lying to Max, and I wouldn't want to disrespect him like that, anyway.

"Want to talk about it?" He adjusted the strap of his mailbag, and I shook my head.

"No, but thank you." I'd told him a bit about my life, but only the surface level things that most people knew. "Would you like some coffee?" I asked as the pot's automatic brew cycle ticked off.

"Sure."

I grabbed a couple of mugs and filled them. "Sugar, creamer, milk, help yourself." Offering him a mug, I added some Irish cream flavored creamer to mine and a teaspoon of sugar. He added a teaspoon of sugar to his and took a sip.

"Hopefully, the day gets better for you. I'm up to my eyeballs in mail, but I always have time for our little chats. You know, I had been thinking about our last conversation, the one where you told me how you were in the National Guard Reserve before becoming the sheriff. Which, by the way, you are the best one this town has ever seen." He took another sip of his coffee as the breeze picked up through the open door.

I moved over to close it and struggled against the urge to lock the deadbolts.

"Anyway, I was thinking about how that training probably helped you to be such a good sheriff. You give this town strength when we feel powerless." He stared off into some point in the distance, and I knew he saw something I couldn't. "But knowing we have someone we can trust watching over us, knowing that our local law enforcement has our backs, and simply knowing that you don't think force is the answer to every issue ... well, you're exactly what the town needs."

"Thank you, Max." His words warmed me up, and I couldn't hold back a slight smile.

"They say that sometimes the people who've been through the darkest times have the most empathy and compassion for others who are suffering." He took another drink of his coffee. I followed suit with a nod.

I agreed with him; the world could be an ugly place, but sometimes that pushed people to the light instead of more darkness.

"I was thinking about that this morning. Feeling powerless." He stared down into his cup as if the coffee within held all the answers.

"Do you ever feel powerless, Max?" I asked, curious.

He nodded. "Sometimes. Some things in life are out of our control. But I also wonder if sometimes we feel powerless because we lock ourselves in prisons of our own making." His words trailed off, and I blinked at the profound thought.

"Anyway, I don't want to hold you up, and I have more deliveries to make." He smiled at me, drank down the rest of his coffee, and placed the mug in the sink.

"Thank you for stopping in. It's always great to chat." I smiled at him, grateful for our talk over coffee.

"Oh, the pleasure is all mine." He gave me a quick around-the-shoulder hug before heading for the door. He hesitated, then turned to me. "I'm here if you need an ear."

I nodded. Max was the keeper of secrets and a person the town could count on for wisdom. "The offer goes both ways," I said.

"Thank you," he said with a smile before letting himself out and closing the door behind him.

My walkie crackled. "Miranda, we have a disturbance on main."

I grabbed my keys and headed out the door, careful to lock it behind me. "Details?" I asked as I headed for the Tahoe.

"There's a protest about Benji outside the paper. He called in and said he's scared." Delilah couldn't sound more bored as she relayed the information, but I took it as seriously as I did any other call.

"I'm on my way." I got behind the wheel and pulled out of the garage, stopping only to make sure the garage door closed before turning out onto the open road. Benji's actions had led to people being upset with him, but never protests. Given the other calls like this I'd had, it was likely one elderly lady yelling at him from the curb as she walked by, telling him some variation of *shame on you for what you did to Kandra!*

Still, I wasn't making any assumptions until I knew the facts. As I drove into town, Bayden played a starring role in my daydreams, and a smile crossed my lips. *Get it together. You cannot possibly entertain this schoolgirl crush; it would never work.*

On Main Street, I saw no signs of a protest, but I saw Norman and Ethel sitting on a bench. I parked, got out, and casually strolled over to them.

"What are you troublemakers up to?" I asked.

Ethel laughed and elbowed Norman. "Hear that? We're *troublemakers.*"

Norman chuckled and stared up at me. "Well, Sheriff, we may have told Benji what we thought about his little stunt with Kandra."

I nodded. I doubted there were any threats from these two, but I also didn't think they'd be nice for the sake of it. "Are you enjoying the sunshine this morning?" I asked.

"Norman was winded, so we sat." Ethel lifted both shoulders.

"Take all the time you need," I placed a hand on Norman's shoulder. It was a public bench on public property. There was no need to ask them to leave. I headed toward the paper and opened the front door where Benji met me with crossed arms and too much attitude.

"You're going to arrest them, right?"

I lifted my eyebrows. "Norman and Ethel?"

He nodded. "They followed me from my car to the front door, telling me that what I did was unforgivable. Then they sat outside, and now they're waiting for me to come out so they can harass me again."

I sighed. "Have they done anything like this before?"

He shook his head.

This whole situation with Benji had proven to be exhausting. "Benji, they're not breaking any laws. They're on public property and allowed to tell you what they think about your actions. That does not make it harassment. If they follow you home or anywhere else, please let me know. If they make threats against you or voice wishes to harm you, then I need to know that too."

"What happened to freedom of the press?" His arms tightened across his chest.

"You're free to print what you like; I won't stop you. However, people are also free to voice their opinions about what you print." This tired argument was one I'd be happy never to hear again. "Look, you aired someone's dirty laundry, and it upset people. They have that right. However, they're not allowed to attack you, threaten you, follow you, or otherwise harass you."

"So, you won't do anything?" His anger shone through in his words, but I kept my cool and responded.

"I'll file a report, but there's nothing more for me to do."

CHAPTER EIGHT

BAYDEN

"Ugh, I'm so freaking excited." Quinn seemed to vibrate as if an electric current was running through him.

As much as I hated to admit it, I was as jumpy and impatient for the news as he was. Last night we'd all gotten the word that Kandra had gone into labor. Noah, sounding stunned and afraid, had told us on a group call that he'd be missing work today.

We'd congratulated him, wished him luck and strength, and all of us were on pins and needles waiting for more news.

"Does it always take this long?" Ethan stalked up behind us, and Quinn lifted both shoulders.

"I don't know, man."

All at once, our phones rang. With significant, excited glances at one another, we all answered to Noah's tired voice. "He's here! Room 206."

"On our way!" Quinn hung up and bolted for his truck. Ethan and I followed and rushed to our vehicles.

"I'll get Mom." I climbed in my truck as Quinn waved, and Ethan flashed a thumbs-up. We all took off. My brothers turned toward the next major town en route to the hospital, but I turned toward my childhood home to pick up Mom.

Pulling up in front of the house, I jumped out and rushed up the steps. Mom met me at the door with a kiss. "I was getting ready to go." Her eyes glittered with joy, and I nodded.

"I'll drive. Let's go!" I grabbed her bag and took her arm before walking her toward my truck. We hurried, and I helped her climb in the passenger side before closing the door and jogging around the truck's front to climb in.

"So how have you been?" she asked.

I snorted. "Mom, seriously. Noah and Kandra had a baby. It's not about me right now." I pulled away from the curb, and she gave me that infamous side-eye look that called bullshit on my attempt to divert attention away from myself.

"Well, we aren't at the hospital yet, so, in the meantime, why don't you tell me how you are doing?"

I sighed. "I'm good. Working. Sleeping well. Behaving and staying out of trouble. You know, the usual." She wouldn't let up until I gave her what she wanted.

She let out a slight, "*Huh.*"

I glanced at her. "What?"

"Oh, nothing. Just that trespassing out on the old farm isn't my idea of staying out of trouble." Her lips twitched and broke into a smile.

How the hell did she know that? "Okay, but I haven't been arrested." I knew better than to play semantics games with my mother. As I pulled out of town onto the freeway, I wondered if Miranda had told her. More likely, Ethel had caught on to my little game and had a conversation with my mother.

"But it is a great way to get to spend time with the sheriff, right?"

I groaned. "Mom, please." Was nothing sacred or private anymore? As I merged into traffic, I heard her laugh as she patted my knee lightheartedly.

"She's a beautiful woman, who's fierce and independent. She'll give you a run for your money, but you would be great together." Mom's approval shone through in her voice, and I struggled against disgust.

"Okay, okay, thank you. You know, your daughter-in-law gave birth to your first grandchild. Let's talk about that." None of us gave a damn that Noah wasn't the child's biological father. The little one was her grandchild, and our nephew, end of story. Blood meant nothing. The baby was family.

"I'm proud of you, Bayden. I know you're intensely private about your love life, and that's okay. Know that I'm here if you need to talk or if you want to talk. You don't have to do this alone." Her soft tone and warmth squeezed my windpipe.

"Thanks, Mom. I know." I took the exit and followed the signs to the hospital. As I pulled into the parking area, I saw my brothers' trucks and found a spot. Once parked, I helped Mom out of the truck, and we headed for the door.

"Room 206," I said, and Mom nodded.

We knocked on the door to the room, and it slid open. Noah smiled and pulled Mom into a hug before squeezing me around the shoulder with one arm.

"You look like shit," I told him in a joking tone.

"Thanks." Despite his attitude, I could feel the humor radiating off him. Under his eyes, the dark circles told me he hadn't slept, and he looked older than his years. No doubt, it was because of the stress of welcoming a new baby into the world. However, the joy in his features was undeniable.

Mom gave me a look and walked toward Kandra. The two talked, and Kandra handed off the little bundle of blankets. Mom took the little one gently, her face filled with awe and love.

"Where'd Quinn and Ethan go?" I asked.

"I sent them for food."

I laughed. "That bad, huh?"

Noah rubbed a hand on the back of his neck with a sheepish look on his face. "Let's say they're a bit excited."

I nodded. "They haven't shut up about this all day." I didn't blame them; this was likely the most exciting thing to happen to any of us in, well, *ever*. "What did you name him?"

Noah glanced at his wife and newborn son, cradled in our mother's arms. "Kip William Lockhart after both our fathers."

My chest tightened. "That's a damn good name. Dad would be proud." I clapped him on the shoulder and headed for Mom. Peeking over her shoulder at the squished-faced baby, I couldn't hold back a smile.

"How are you?" I asked Kandra.

She flashed me a tired smile. "Good. I'm glad you're all here."

"Is your mother on her way?" Mom asked.

"She's actually out of town, but we've sent pictures and videos already." Kandra's sad voice brightened as little Kip wiggled and sighed. The door slid open to show my brothers.

"Pizza!" Quinn set the boxes down, and Ethan set the sodas on the counter.

"And drinks. Dig in, Noah." Ethan walked up to Mom and me to peek down at the little sleeping one. "He's so dang cute."

Kandra's smile grew, but Mom seemed lost in the moment, and she didn't even respond.

"Well, we're never getting a turn to hold the baby, so maybe we should leave and let Mom take him home." I winked at Kandra, who chuckled.

"I would never," Mom said, glancing up at me.

"Then you won't mind if I..." I reached out and gently took the baby from her. Supporting his little head with one hand and his body with the other, I lifted him to my chest. I'd swear everyone was holding their breath, and I wanted to flip them all off. "Oh, come on, I know how to hold a baby." I cradled him close and gently rocked him, wrapping an arm under his body and holding his head. He opened his little bright-blue eyes, squinted at me, yawned, and then went back to sleep.

"My turn?" Quinn crept up on me, arms out.

I pulled the baby back and growled at him. "Get your own."

"He's not yours."

Kandra and Noah laughed. I continued to rock Kip for a few moments, telling him I'd be the world's best uncle and not to worry about Quinn or Ethan. They were okay but not as great as I'd be.

"You should call Miranda," Mom said, then glanced at Kandra. "I mean, if you two are okay with it."

Kandra nodded. "Invite her. I know you two are getting kind of serious."

I passed the baby carefully to Quinn while wondering if everyone in town knew about the sheriff and me. "Where did you hear that?" It only felt right for her to be here for my family event because I was happy and wanted to share that with her.

"It doesn't matter where I heard it because it is written all over your face. You know we don't care if she joins us, if she wants to." Kandra smiled at me as she called me out, but I wasn't upset.

"Okay, okay, I'll call her." I pulled my phone out of my pocket and headed for the door. The buzz of voices brought a smile to my lips as my family talked about the baby. Meanwhile, I was thinking of the holidays and all the fun we could have. I was excited to teach Kip to swim, to play horse, to climb trees.

And it hit me; *Holy hell. Do I want to be a dad?*

I shook off the thought. I wasn't even in a relationship; I had no business thinking about fatherhood for myself. I dialed Miranda's number, and she picked up on the second ring.

"Hello?"

Her voice widened my smile. "Hey, I'm an uncle."

"Congratulations." Her warm tone heated me right up.

"He's a little boy named Kip William Lockhart." I could hear the excitement bleeding through in my voice, and she laughed.

"I love that name."

I sat down in the little waiting room near the window in hopes of better reception. "Thank you. They named him after our dad and after Kandra's dad."

"How is Kandra?" Her supportive, friendly voice was music to my ears, and I realized that, as always, I enjoyed talking to her. Calling her for this event felt right, and I was glad I'd done so.

"She's good! Tired, I think. They both are; it was a long night." I thought about the exhaustion in my brother's eyes and how worn out Kandra looked. That was to be expected, though, they'd been up all night bringing a life into the world.

"They wanted you to know that you're more than welcome to come to visit." I held my breath, wondering if my original gut feeling was right. Was this too weird? Too familiar? I mean, we were friends, but were we this close? Miranda didn't strike me as the baby-crazy kind of woman who'd be in for anything because there's a baby involved.

"That's so sweet." The distance in her voice bothered me. It was as if we were suddenly strangers instead of friends, and potentially more, discussing this life-changing event.

"Yeah, Kandra sees you as family. We all do." Everyone welcomed Miranda into the family with open arms. That's how we'd always been. Anyone important to me was important to all of them.

"Thank you." Her voice sounded choked, and I wondered if I'd done or said something wrong.

"We're at Cypress. Room 206." I felt like I was desperately clutching at straws trying to get her to come, but something in me whispered that she wouldn't. I didn't understand why, but I'd respect her decision, regardless.

"Thank you for the invite. I appreciate it." An odd note infiltrated her voice, something I couldn't identify, but it bothered me.

I didn't know what to say. "I'm not sure exactly what the visiting hours are." I wanted to kick myself for being so clumsy.

"I don't think I'm going to come there, but the offer touches me." Her upbeat tone hid something darker, something I couldn't put my finger on.

"Okay, no worries. I just wanted you to know you're welcome to visit and meet the little cutie. I still can't believe I'm an uncle. We're going to have so much fun." My smile widened as I thought about all the ways I could spoil my nephew. That was the point, right? Spoil him and send him home?

"He's lucky to have you. Anyway, I have to go." Her odd inflection didn't ease up, and the line went dead in my ear.

Confused, I stared at the phone in my hand.

CHAPTER NINE

MIRANDA

I knew I'd hung up too abruptly. I had no doubt that Bayden would call me back and ask what was going on. I'd have to ignore the call because there was no way I could explain myself. There was no way I could tell him the truth about my sister or my past. I couldn't tell him or anyone else.

I shoved my phone in my pocket, hating that my hands were shaking. Grabbing the steering wheel, I gripped it until the seams of the leather wrapping squeaked in protest. Drawing in a deep breath, I let it out slowly, then took another, and another.

And the world whirled and tilted.

Forcing myself to breathe normally, I stared at the street, struggling to calm myself down. A few people walked by, including Norman and Ethel. They smiled and waved, and I nodded and waved right back. I could only hope they didn't notice my distress, though I thought the tinted windows would keep my secret safe.

I was happy for the Lockhart family. I knew how excited Kandra and Noah were to be having a baby. I loved that Bayden was proud to be an uncle. I had no doubts he'd be a great uncle too. The child would know love, unconditional care, and a stable support system that would allow him to thrive. The little one would have everything he needed for a solid start in life, and I knew he could accomplish anything he set out to with that kind of force behind them.

But it also meant whatever feelings existed between Bayden and me were going to be more difficult, if not downright impossible. I didn't want to be an aunt. I wanted nothing to do with a baby. I wanted nothing to do with children in general. And he'd made it clear today that he didn't share my views on that point. Where did that leave *us*?

He probably wanted kids. If nothing else, he wanted to be an uncle. I didn't even want to be an aunt, let alone a mother. It was one of those deal-breakers that ruined relationships. I couldn't ask him not to have kids or see his nephew while I was around. I wouldn't make him choose between us. That would make me a monster, but forcing myself to be around kids would be torture.

Tears stung my eyes as my knuckles went white, and the feeling left my fingers. I'd known this was coming, but I guess I hoped he'd be indifferent to kids or that maybe I could warm up to the idea. The genuine panic gnawing at my guts told me neither outcome was possible. Twin tears rolled down my cheeks.

I wasn't the nurturing or mothering type. I didn't have the skills, ability, or drive to want to be around children at all. I knew this meant I was going to lose Bayden, and that thought clamped down on my heart like a vise. This was the final straw; the beginning of the end of our relationship, and I wouldn't even be able to explain why: why I'm broken, why I am no good for him, why he should be with someone who knows how to love and accept love.

Memories surged forward, refusing to be ignored. I closed my eyes, hoping for darkness, but instead, I saw *her* face—my sister's beautiful face. Pain roared through me, blazing like white-hot fire, igniting every inch of my skin and filling my lungs with brimstone as I inhaled.

I turned over the engine and headed home. My shift was over, and I needed to escape everything. I'd shower up and head to Roy's. It seemed like a good night for a few drinks.

ROY BROUGHT me a beer and hesitated as if he had something to say.

"Everything okay?" he asked.

I nodded. "I'd also like an order of garlic knots if you're cooking," I said with a grateful smile. I knew I needed something solid in my stomach, or I'd be asking someone to drive me home.

"Coming right up. Anything else?" His kind eyes searched my face, and I shook my head.

"That's perfect, thank you." Struggling to keep my tone upbeat, I settled into my seat. He walked off, and I let my shoulders droop. My life was a crumbling mess. I could run from my past, but life had repeatedly proven that the past would only follow me. No matter how far I went, and no matter how I tried to atone for my mistakes, nothing would fix things.

Helpless, I picked up my beer with a tired smile and took a sip. I reminded myself to go easy on it until the bread hit the table. I didn't want to wind up drunk. An empty stomach plus beer was a recipe for disaster.

The door opened, and instantly, the mood of the room changed. An electric charge filled the air, and the hairs on my arms and the back of my neck stood on end. I glanced up and locked eyes with Benji as people in the bar murmured.

Roy stepped out and gestured for Benji to leave. "You're not welcome here."

Benji pointed to me. "I need to talk to the sheriff."

"She's off duty. Leave her alone."

I stood up and gestured *it's okay* at Roy, who relaxed. "I can step outside to talk with him." I moved toward Benji, but Roy was quick to speak up.

"I'd rather you talk to him in here, so we can keep an eye on things." Roy's distaste and mistrust of Benji were evident.

"It's up to you." I glanced at Roy, who signaled for Benji to come inside. I sat back down amidst the murmurs. "This better be important." If Benji tried to stir things up or use me in some game he was playing, I didn't have the energy to put up with him. "Roy has every right not to want you here."

"Are you ready to talk to me, yet?"

I snorted. This routine was getting old. "Why would I do that? After what you did to Kandra, you think I'm going to talk to you?"

He sighed and sat next to me. "Look, I was out of line, and I'm sorry."

"Which time?" He'd been out of line plenty of times, and I was curious about which time he was referring.

"All of them. I shouldn't have messed with Kandra. I knew Norman and Ethel weren't in the wrong, but all of this is wearing on me, you know? Everyone hates me." He gestured around the bar, and I held back the urge to chuckle and say something like *actions have consequences*. I knew that kind of response wouldn't help, so I kept it to myself.

"Okay, let's say you're sorry. If I refuse to talk to you, are you going to dig for dirt on me too? I think I cheated on a test in third grade. Want to tell everyone about that?" I didn't feel bad for him. I'd do my job and keep him safe, but I wasn't his friend.

Roy put garlic knots in front of me, and I thanked him. Tearing one of the buttery bread bites off the bunch, I dipped it in the homemade marinara sauce and popped it into my mouth. The bread's hot perfection was heavenly, and the bitter bite of garlic and creamy butter hit the spot after my hard day.

"Look," Benji said, before pressing his lips into a thin line.

I glanced at him curiously. The Benji I knew would never hold back or shut up if he had something to say.

His shoulders drooped, and his head sagged.

"I admit it. I screwed up."

I resisted the urge to roll my eyes. It was too little, too late. If he meant it, why had he been doubling down on all his bullshit since he ran the piece? Why not issue a retraction and apology if he believed he'd done something wrong? "Everybody makes mistakes."

I guessed giving credit where credit was due was important. He was admitting he'd screwed up.

I took a sip of my beer.

"Yeah, but this was a big mistake. I don't really have friends. I saw Kandra slipping away forever, and I did something stupid, and now I'm being punished for it. I don't know how to fix it." A vulnerable note entered his voice, and I sat up and took notice.

I needed to put aside my own opinions and thoughts of him. He was asking for help, even if he didn't realize it. I could hear it, and I needed to treat him with the same respect and care I'd treat anyone else in a difficult situation.

"Have you considered a public apology? Maybe a retraction on the article?" I took another bite of garlic bread and glanced at him. He'd put his head down on the table and stared forward like a sad puppy into the distance.

"I thought about it, but would anyone listen? Would anyone believe me?" He sounded lost and broken.

"Even if no one believes you, would you feel better if you did the right thing?" I took a sip of my beer, and he lifted his head to study my face for a second.

"I hadn't thought about that." His tone shifted as if his whole perspective was changing. I wouldn't hold my breath, but I hoped he was taking this to heart.

"I'm going to tell you this, and if you use it for evil, I'll never trust you again," I spoke slowly and clearly. "Their son was born today. I think if you issued an apology and a beautiful birth announcement congratulating them, you might earn back some credibility. Before you do, I'd make sure you mean what you say and that you nail this. Otherwise, it'll come across poorly. If you use this against me, we'll have problems, okay?"

He nodded. "Thank you for talking to me." He didn't say it, and he didn't need to add that no one else would speak to him. He turned to the bar as he rose. "Thank you, Roy." He nodded at Roy, who glared at him until he left the bar.

"You okay?" Roy asked.

"I'm okay, Roy. Thank you for being patient."

He nodded, and I continued eating my bread and drinking my beer. As I did, my mind shifted to those unwanted places, and an overwhelming sense of dread filled me once more. I could help other people with their problems, but I would slowly drown in mine.

"I hope he didn't ruin your night." Gypsy moved to my table and sat next to me, a smile on her face as the sage's earthy smell chased her over.

I offered a smile I didn't feel. "Oh, no, Benji doesn't have that kind of power in my life."

"Good. How is Bayden?"

I gulped my beer.

The people in this town didn't quit, did they?

CHAPTER TEN

BAYDEN

I glanced at my phone again. Miranda hadn't been responding to texts or calls, and I was going nuts. I'd given her the rest of yesterday in peace. I knew something was wrong because she never hung up that quickly.

I assumed she needed space. I didn't want to crowd her or stress her out, but now it was Wednesday, and she still wasn't responding. I paced back and forth. Last time I'd showed up at her place, bad things happened. I was hesitant to do that again.

I lifted my phone and called her number. It rang once. Twice. Three times. Then the call went to voicemail. I hung up and continued pacing.

"Damn it." I couldn't handle not knowing if she'd made it home safe from work the previous day or not knowing that she was okay. She'd sounded so off on the phone yesterday.

Grabbing my keys off the counter, I headed to my truck. I couldn't deal with this overwhelming sense of fear and dread that something might have happened to her. All I knew was that if I didn't find out how she was doing, I would lose my mind.

There wasn't much crime in our little town, but that didn't mean she couldn't wind up hurt. Accidents happened. And given that she was typically responsive to my calls and messages, this was stressing me the hell out.

I climbed into my truck and was on the road in two minutes. The drive was plagued with thoughts of what might have happened to her. *A car accident? A slip in the shower?* I knew how tired she could be after those double shifts, and since I didn't know her exact schedule, I had no way of knowing what days she was working them.

Maybe I was being stupid and overthinking or overreacting, but something didn't feel right. My gut told me I needed to worry about her, and I would trust that feeling.

I pulled in front of her place and killed the engine in her driveway. Trying to keep calm, I hurried up to her front door and knocked.

No answer.

I knocked again, making a plan for if she didn't answer. I could check the garage for the Tahoe. If she was home, I could check doors and windows to see if anything was unlocked. I'd find a way to get to her and make sure she was safe. I'd deal with whatever consequences came with my actions when I knew for sure she was okay.

There was no answer, and I backed up a step and studied the house, looking for any sign of activity. I made it off the steps to check the garage when the door opened.

I turned to face her, stunned by her appearance. Dark shadows under her eyes reminded me of bruises. Her look of confusion bothered me, and her tousled hair led me to believe I'd woken her up. It was noon.

She grabbed my collar and tugged at me. "Are you okay?"

Without responding, she stepped back into her house, pulling me along.

"It worried me that you weren't answering my texts or calls. And after how our conversation ended yesterday..." I didn't know what else to say as she pulled me inside and closed the door behind me.

She hadn't said a single word, but she locked the three deadbolts on the door before gripping the fabric of my shirt again.

"Are you okay, Miranda?" Something didn't feel right. The quiet was unlike her. The glossy look in her eyes reminded me of something I couldn't quite place. "Miranda?"

She continued tugging me, and I went with her, powerless to stop the momentum. *What the hell is going on?*

I thought coming to see her would ease some of my worries, but this was only making me more concerned. "Miranda?"

She stopped pulling me when we reached her living room. Cool tones decorated the comfortable space. I only knew that because of the dozens of times we had to deal with designers. Miranda's color palette was distinctly cool with the gray couch, charcoal-colored wood flooring, and deep gray accent wall. If not for the large open window that let in the light, it would be like a cave. I noticed something strange about the window; it was nailed shut.

The three deadbolts on the door, combined with her odd behavior, proved something wasn't right.

She pulled me back toward the couch, and I went with her, worried and confused about what was happening. She still hadn't said a word, and the look in her eyes was almost ... *vacant*. Her place held a hint of her perfume and coffee, a familiar combination that reminded me of home.

It was the first time I'd been inside her house, and while it was comfortable and appealing, something was making the hairs on the back of my neck stand on end.

She pulled me back, back, back, lowering herself onto the couch and bringing me down. Her lips met mine, and her arms wound around my shoulders.

Stunned, I froze as her tongue slipped past my lips.

Everything in me wanted to respond. Memories of our night together and our kisses filled me. Heat blazed through every inch of my body, but this wasn't the Miranda I knew. Although this was a side of Miranda I was eager to meet.

"Kiss me," she whispered.

That was all the permission I needed. Miranda's legs parted for me, and I pressed down between her thighs and kissed her. Tangling my fingers in her hair, my lips continued to caress hers to the point she was gasping for air. I lifted some of my weight and pressure off her in case I was too heavy, and I growled a little as I deepened the kiss even more. My mind was no longer in charge, and my animalistic instincts seemed to take over.

My whole body demanded more, but I knew I had to keep it in check. Miranda was so delicious, willing, open, and sweet, but there was still a nagging feeling that something wasn't quite right. Her kiss was different—almost lazy. It was as if she wasn't genuinely taking part. Though she started the kiss, it seemed more like I was leading now, and she was surrendering. There was no fire inside her. The lack of spark I'd expect from a woman as strong as Miranda killed the lust growing within me.

I pulled back and sat beside her. She froze, legs spread, her short shorts clinging to her skin, and the tank top clearly showing she was wearing nothing under it. So I wouldn't stare, I glanced away.

"Are you okay?" I looked at her again, this time keeping my eyes on her face.

She blinked, and some cloudiness seemed to clear. She sat up, pulling her legs to her chest and winding her arms around them as she shook her head as if to clear it further.

"You kissed me," I said, a smile on my lips. I was trying to bring some lighthearted fun into the moment. I wanted to put her at ease and tried to peel away the tension clinging to the situation.

Her fingers pressed to her lips as if she could still feel mine on hers. The last of the cobwebs seemed to clear, and she sat up. She glanced down at what she was wearing, then stood.

"Coffee?" she asked as if she could blow off what transpired between us without an explanation.

I wasn't about to let that happen, but coffee sounded good.

"Yes, please." I stood and followed her, but she ducked into a room, and the door swung closed. A moment later, she popped out in a strappy, flowing dress without the tank top under it. Her back, neck, shoulders, and part of her chest were exposed, but the dress looked causal and kind of sexy.

"I've never seen you in a dress," I said, impressed.

She shrugged. "It's comfortable around the house."

"So ... you kissed me." I followed her into the kitchen.

"I have ... episodes."

I chuckled. "Random kissing episodes?"

She waved a hand at me like I was an idiot, and maybe I was.

"No, they're like sleepwalking, but not quite. My body and mind still think I'm dreaming, but I'm up moving around."

Suddenly things made sense.

"That's why you have three deadbolts and a window nailed shut? You might want to consider something more effective, since you let me in so easily. Just saying." I said teasingly. "But in all seriousness, it's not a deal-breaker, just so you know. I mean, if you're kissing every person who winds up on your doorstep, maybe, but sleep-walking isn't going to send me running."

She tensed up but continued to gather things to make coffee. I watched her measure the grounds, and when she turned around to face me, I sensed something still wasn't right—my need to fix things kicked in. I was a fixer and a pleaser and a teaser. Those were some of my superpowers. I had others, but I'd have to get her naked to show off those skills.

"Are you telling me you dream about kissing me?" I arched a brow, and her lips twitched. "Because if you were dreaming and pulling me into the house and onto the couch and begging me to kiss you—"

"I didn't beg you!"

Her indignant tone didn't help her case, and I held back a smile while leaning in close and whispering. "Kiss me."

She laughed and pushed me away. "It's not my fault."

"No one would blame you for wanting to kiss me. How often do you dream about locking lips with me?" I loved razzing her, especially when her cheeks heated to a delicate pink color.

She shook her head and turned back to the mugs she'd taken out of the cabinet. "We are not having this conversation."

"Oh, you dream about kissing me all the time." I stepped in so close I could smell her fresh scent and the hint of coconut in her hair. Gently grabbing her hips, I leaned in close. "Would you say every night?"

"Stop it." She pushed me away with a laugh, and I couldn't help but mimic the sound.

"If it makes you feel better, I think about kissing you too." It wasn't a lie. I was head over heels for this girl, and I knew it. Even finding out about her odd sleep issues didn't deter me or diminish my desire for her company.

"I'm sure you do," she said, rolling her eyes with an exasperated—though playful—sigh. "I'm sorry I worried you."

"I'm sorry I intruded on you like this, and that I didn't realize something was up sooner. I apologize for letting things progress beyond what you might have been comfortable with." The nagging thought that things could have gone further between us worried me. When I made love to Miranda, I wanted her to be present.

Her cheeks went from pink to red. "Well, let me assure you that if things had gone further, I wouldn't be upset."

The words hit me like a baseball bat to the daddy bag, and I exhaled a slow, painful breath. I'd let that comment go and would think more about it later.

"Sorry, the honesty seemed necessary. You don't need that kind of guilt knocking around upstairs." She tapped my temple with a gentle fingertip.

"No, it's fine." My voice sounded too strained for her to believe.

The aroma of coffee filled my nose, and she quickly poured both mugs. While she prepared hers, I took a sip of mine. The hot sting helped move the thoughts and blood away from my belt region and back to my brain. "You look like you haven't been sleeping well."

"You're right. I have trouble sleeping sometimes. It comes and goes in waves." It was the most candid she'd been with me, and I liked it. We headed into the living room and settled on the couch with our coffee.

"You wouldn't believe all the places my head went from car accidents to shower slips," I needed to clarify that comment. "I know you get tired after those double shifts, and stuff can happen."

She nodded and then stared at my lips. "Bayden, I want you to kiss me again."

CHAPTER ELEVEN

MIRANDA

Bayden cleared his throat, lowering his coffee.

"Nobody likes black coffee." I nodded at his cup, and he lifted his shoulders.

"Considering our conversation, I could take a double shot of something stronger." He peered into the cup as if it contained all the answers, and I couldn't help but tease him a little.

"Like espresso? I don't have anything that fancy." He meant liquor, but I enjoyed seeing him off balance. It was unlike the Bayden I thought I knew. He'd always been a confident-leap-before-looking type, but he was oddly delicate with this subject.

He shook his head and took another sip. "You know, I've never even had an espresso."

His gaze met mine, and I tried to figure out if the turn the conversation had taken made him change his mind about kissing me again.

I resisted the urge to let my shoulders curl forward and pulled them back to sit up taller.

"I have, but only the ones out of a can. They're good, unlike energy drinks. Those things taste like battery acid." I smiled and took another drink of my coffee. The Irish cream dulled the bitter coffee, and the last remnants of sleep cleared like fog burned off by sunshine.

He nodded, leaning back and showing off those powerful arms and shoulders of his. Curiosity filled me. What would he do if I leaned in and kissed him? I wasn't modest or a prude by any stretch, but I wasn't sure that pressing my luck was a good idea. My push and pull behavior was likely giving him whiplash.

"I don't drink energy drinks; bad for the heart." Sadness edged into his eyes, and I wondered if there was some painful memory there. I didn't want to dredge any of that up at the moment, so I nodded silently instead.

"Are you hungry?" I asked him. Unable to help myself, I added, "I mean, when you wake up with someone, isn't it customary to fix them breakfast?" With a wicked smile, I watched him choke on his coffee.

"We woke up together?"

I lifted a shoulder. "Kind of. I mean, you were here when I woke up. I would have liked that to have started and ended differently." While I was feeling bold, I continued. "It's no secret that I'm attracted to you. We went on a date. We're both adults. There is a natural progression to things, right? Sex and waking up together is part of that." Was my lack of knowledge in this department backfiring on me? I'd never held down a serious relationship before.

He nodded. "You're right. I guess I didn't have expectations. Hope, yes. Expectations, no."

"Disappointed that it went differently?" I was asking because I wasn't sure he was.

He shook his head. "No, not at all." With a smile, he took another drink. His cologne tickled my nose, and I breathed him in. I wanted him to kiss me again. I did. His kisses were heated and passionate and made my heart beat a little too fast.

But it was wrong, too. I was leading him on because I knew there was no way we could be together. His wants and needs were too much for me. We desired different things out of life, and to continue pushing forward was dishonest and cruel if I could never give him what he wanted and needed. The selfish side of me wanted him just once, even though I knew I wouldn't be good for him. Still, I craved another kiss. Surely, one more couldn't hurt.

However, something was off, and he knew it. But instead of pressing forward like most men would, he stopped. Sex wasn't the only thing on his mind because he *cared* for me.

Someone so intuitive had to be a fantastic lover.

The fact I liked him a lot didn't help clear up the confusion swirling inside me. I wanted to be with him, and not only for kissing and sex. There were certain parts I couldn't handle—kids. I wasn't ready to explain my family situation and didn't want to cheat him out of something so important. I knew how much family meant to him, and not having one of my own to bring into his life would be unkind.

"You're thinking some heavy thoughts."

I glanced up as my teeth bit into my lower lip, and I sucked on the stinging flesh.

"Yeah." I smiled at him, then continued to worry my lip.

"Want to talk about it?" His soft expression warmed me right up,

"No," I said, then I leaned forward and pressed my lips to his.

He stiffened, then relaxed as I wound my arms around his broad shoulders. His hands found and rested on my hips as his warmth sank through the thin material of my dress and into my skin. The contact encouraged me to lean closer until I pressed myself firmly to his body. Excitement flared through me, and I let out a soft mewling sound.

"Are you sure you want this?" he spoke against my lips.

My voice stuck in my throat, so I whispered my response. "I'm sure." I'd never been so sure of something in my life. Shoving aside that little nagging voice that told me this was wrong and I should stop, I kissed him again.

His arms felt like home, and the coffee flavor on his tongue added a different richness to the kiss. My entire body hummed with desire, and I gave in to the overwhelming sensations.

I leaned back for a second. Bayden's questioning gaze cleared up as I offered him my hand. His warm fingers wrapped around mine, and I rose and led him through the house toward my bed.

In my room, I turned to face him. Pulling him in closer until the bed was behind us, I gave him a gentle push. The fire in his eyes and the hunger in his features had my stomach flipping and falling. Without hesitation, I moved in and straddled his lap while he sat there on the end of my bed, his arms planted behind him for support.

Whatever was between us wasn't going away. It had to run its course. I just hoped we wouldn't crash and burn.

Loving the warmth of him and the thrill of straddling his lap, I attacked his mouth like a starving woman. His pants did nothing to hide his arousal, and that sent my pulse racing until all I could hear was the pumping of blood in my ears.

He pulled back. "Are you nervous?" he whispered.

I swallowed hard. "Does it show?" I'd been doing my best to be calm and in charge.

"You're trembling." His eyes met mine before lowering to my lips again.

"I'm a little nervous." Saying the words out loud eased the tension knotting me up. "But I don't want to stop." The physical intimacy wasn't the problem; my secrets and the fact that I wanted more than sex with him but knew we were incompatible as a couple were the problems.

Shoving those troubling thoughts aside, I pressed a hand flat to his chest and pushed him gently. He took the hint and relaxed on his back, looking up at me with undisguised lust.

I peeled my dress up and over my head and tossed it aside. Turning back to him, I caught the stunned look on his face as he took in my nakedness. "You're looking at me like you've never seen someone naked before."

"If that were true, I could die a happy man only ever having seen you." His whisper did something to my insides, and I melted. Bayden was pure temptation. It should have been a crime for him to say something so sweet. He gave me something I hadn't had in a lifetime

... hope. Hope was a dangerous thing for a woman like me. Hope made the impossible seem possible when I knew it could never be.

Being with him like this should have been uncomfortable or embarrassing. I mean, how long had it been since someone saw me naked? But I didn't feel awkward or worried. With Bayden, I felt safe and warm and loved.

I let out a squeal as he bucked, rolling us over on my bed. With his body leaning over me, I felt intoxicated as I gasped with anticipation. He reared up and peeled off his shirt. I sat up to run my hands up the expanse of his well-defined pecs. At the touch of my fingers, his muscles bunched and coiled. The guy was built like a gladiator, and I wanted to kiss every inch of him.

He leaned forward and grazed my lips with his. His belt clanked slightly, and the sound sent electric tingles through me. A moment later, the sound of a foil wrapper tearing filled me with warmth. I watched as he rolled it on.

He lowered himself on top of me, and I wound around him. My arms looped his shoulders, while my legs tucked around his hips with my ankles locked behind his thighs.

As he pressed into me, his tongue worked circles around mine. I let out a whimper at the overwhelming sensations. Our bodies fit and moved like we were made for one another. For a second, I wondered if maybe we could make it work. I mean, he used protection. It's not like he was hell-bent on kids right now.

I buried that notion because someday he would. Clinging to him as tears stung my eyes, I let myself get lost: in him, his touch, the ache in my heart, and the heat of the moment.

"You're amazing," I whispered, needing him to know.

He let out a growl and nuzzled into my neck. "And you're perfect."

He was wrong. So very, very wrong.

We moved together as emotions overwhelmed me. Deep down, my heart begged me to make us work even though I knew it wouldn't.

"I need to love you." The low timbre of his voice tightened my core, and I couldn't hold back the pleasure screaming through my body. I clung to him, safer at that moment than I'd ever felt before. He held me, his warmth surrounding me as his skin pressed to mine.

An awful feeling chased the pleasure. He was here with no lies and no half-truths. Now that I'd had a taste of Bayden, could I ever give him up? Could I walk away? The thought hit my heart like a bat to a ball.

He groaned low in his throat, his entire body stiffening. I held him close, burying my face in his shoulder, and filling my lungs with his scent. His heat warmed me; his heartbeat danced with mine, and everything was perfect.

Except ... it wasn't. It was all a beautiful lie.

"Are you okay?"

I nodded, my heart breaking in my chest.

He pressed his forehead to mine. "I know you're struggling," he said, planting a quick kiss on my lips. "But I will always be here for you. I want to be a constant in your life, and I won't waver. You deserve someone who will lift you up and protect you, and I want to be the man for you."

My throat tightened and closed. Bayden was so much more than I could ask for. I will never know why I was lucky enough to receive his devotion, but it wasn't fair for him to be saddled with someone like me. I knew letting him go would be hard, but damn he made it nearly impossible.

Without bothering to pull away, he kept talking in that low, calming voice. "I'll wait as long as you need me to. I'll wait until you're ready to be mine. Please don't try to push me away because I am not going anywhere."

CHAPTER TWELVE

BAYDEN

Miranda grabbed my collar and pulled me in for another quick kiss. "I want to call off work," she whispered, smiling as she stared up into my eyes. I stood by her front door, wanting nothing more than to stay with her. But she had her career, and people depended on her.

"I'd like that, but one of us has to be responsible." I kissed her again, and her smile widened. My time with her had been short, but mind-blowingly incredible. Work called her in for something minor. She didn't share details, and I didn't press.

"Oh, and you're the responsible one?" She leaned her delicious body into me, and the urge to pick her up and carry her back to bed hit me with the force of a runaway freight train.

"You sound like you think I'm irresponsible." I nuzzled my nose into her neck. "I'm sure I talked you into fixing whatever issue they were having."

Her eyebrows lifted. "You talked me into it?"

She would not let me off easy. "Yes. You told me you didn't want to go." Neither of us wanted to untangle out of bed and get up, but I knew her work was critical to her and the town. I didn't want to be the reason she didn't get things done at work.

"Hmm..." she said, winding an arm around my shoulders as if she had no intention of letting me go now or later.

"Get to it, warrior woman." I gave her another kiss and unlocked each of the bolts on the door before stepping out.

Her hand snagged the back of my shirt, and I turned in time to catch her as she flew into my arms. She clung to me, her arms and legs wrapped around me like she was afraid if I left, I'd never return. I loved this playful side of her. Sheriff Miranda differed significantly from the Miranda I had the privilege of enjoying all afternoon.

She finally unwound from my grasp, and I set her gently on her feet. Cupping her cheek, I leaned in slowly and planted one more kiss on her lips. With a smile on my face and a light step, I pivoted and headed for my truck, swinging my keys the whole way. When I glanced back, the smile on her face was broad, but it didn't reach her eyes. There was something sad in her expression that worried me.

I'd meant what I said. I would wait as long as it took for Miranda to come around and tell me what had her so sad. Turning over the engine in my truck, I backed out of the driveway and pointed the tires toward home.

The phone rang, and I answered hands-free. "Hello?"

"Bayden!" Kandra sounded exhausted and happy.

"Uh-oh, I'm not the first person you've called." I didn't care, but the relief in her voice said she'd been trying to get hold of someone, and I was the first to pick up.

"We tried both our moms. After them, you were next." She let out a tired laugh. "Would you mind watching the baby for us? If I don't get a shower and a nap, I'm sure I'll die."

"No need to justify, sis. If you need a break, I'm happy to help. How's Noah?"

"I think he passed out in his chair." Just then, the baby let out a thin wail.

"I'm on my way." I hung up and adjusted the route to head for their house. With a sigh, I reminded myself to be careful. I didn't want my brother or Kandra to catch wind of what Miranda and I had been up to. It was no one else's business, but our own, and I would keep that secret.

A few moments later, I parked behind Noah's truck. The front door opened, and he waved at me. The dark bags under his eyes spoke to how exhausted he was.

"You look like shit, brother," I said as I hopped up the steps and gave him a bear hug.

He patted my shoulder, then pulled back to give me a quizzical stare. "And you're acting weird."

"I get to play uncle." I couldn't hold back my grin. It thrilled me to spend time with my nephew, but I also knew it might be an excellent cover for the other reason I was in a good mood. I slugged his arm and headed inside to find Kandra like she could save me from my brother's suspicions.

She was in the nursery, rocking the baby. Her tired smile told me everything, so I walked up to her, holding out my arms. I took my nephew as she gingerly placed him against my chest. He squirmed, but his eyes stayed closed. Cradling him close, I glanced at her.

"Are you sure you're comfortable with this?" Her tired blue eyes searched my face.

I nodded. "I won't drop him or let him drink and drive."

Her eyes widened.

I laughed. "Relax; I've been around babies before. You have food for him, diapers, changes of clothes, all the things?" I wasn't afraid of babies. When they cried, they needed something. Either to poop, have their butts wiped, or to eat. They were simple if you covered their base needs.

"Yeah, diaper bag," she offered it, and I slung it over my shoulder. She turned to me, and I stopped short. "The milk has to be put in the fridge. Then you have to warm it, but it can't be hot."

I nodded. "I've done this before." After being in a relationship with a single mom, I understood how babies worked. Though we'd gone our separate ways after a few months, we were still friends on social media, and I enjoyed seeing the little tyke growing up.

"Yeah, he dated Marilyn when she had her baby. Whatever happened to her?" Noah stood in the doorway with his arms crossed.

"She moved three states away to live closer to her parents." We'd never been all that serious. "I also know how the car seat works, but if you'd like to set it up..." I gestured with my armful of sleeping baby and shoulder bag, and Noah nodded.

"I'll do that." He left the room, and Kandra gave me the side-eye.

"Did he say anything?" she asked.

Keeping my expression as innocent as I could, I stared at her. "About what?"

She gave me a look that said not to trick her.

I lifted both shoulders while providing a slight, confused shake of my head.

She sighed. "You and Miranda. Did he say anything?"

"No. Why would he?"

She crossed her arms and pressed her lips together. I knew she knew something had happened. "Look," she said, lowering her arms and touching my shoulder, "we're both happy for you guys."

"I'm going to go see how he's doing." Trying to exit as a means to end the conversation didn't happen, though, and she followed me out.

"Call us if there's an issue, okay?" She peeked up at me, the trust in her eyes filling me with warmth.

"For sure, but I want you guys to relax. Enjoy yourselves, enjoy each other. I've got this, I swear." I knew being a new parent was stressful, and I wanted them to decompress.

She nodded, her exhaustion evident with every step. "Thank you for this."

"You're welcome. It's the first of many times, I hope." We walked toward my truck, and Noah popped his head out.

"All done." He gently took his son and put him in the car seat while I put the bag in the passenger's spot. When I turned again, Kandra hugged me, and when she let go, my brother hugged me.

"Keep him safe."

"With my life." I meant every word; family was everything to me. I'd walk across hot coals for any of them and take a bullet to protect Kip.

I waved at them as I backed out of the driveway. "It's you and me now, Kip." I glanced at the rear-facing car seat. The baby let out a slight snort, and I smiled. He slept the whole drive back to my place.

Parked in my driveway, I stared at my empty house, imagining Miranda there with little Kip and me. The thought filled me with happiness. I got out of the truck to get my nephew, grabbing the bag and his car seat, and I carried him inside.

Taking him into the living room, I set the car seat on the floor and gingerly took him out. "What are we going to do, little man?"

But he slumbered on as if that's all he wanted in life. I could relate.

My mind drifted to Miranda, and I wondered how she'd feel about this scene. Something told me she wasn't baby crazy, but given how close we'd gotten, I had a feeling she'd be less wary about getting attached.

It was way too soon to be thinking about her having my child, but the thought of her pregnant and adorable filled my mind. Having a child as beautiful as she was, for me to love and protect, did something strange to my insides.

I shoved those thoughts aside. I had no business thinking about Miranda that way, though I had to admit the idea had a certain appeal. I wanted to settle down and find someone to love forever. I wanted a companion in life, and Miranda was the right choice for me. She was soft and strong, no-nonsense, and compassionate. She was the perfect mix.

Kip wiggled and opened his eyes. He squinted suspiciously at me, yawned too big, and then smacked his lips. His little chin and tongue worked as if he was sucking, and I got up, cradling him close.

"How about we get you a snack?" I grabbed the bag and dug inside it with one hand to find the milk and put the sealed bottles in the fridge except for one. "This is hard to do with you here." I brought him into the living room, put him in his car seat, and then carried it into the kitchen.

"You know, we're going to have so much fun together."

He wasn't even looking at me, but I didn't mind. "We're going to go to fairs, hiking, swimming, fishing, all the things my dad did with me." My chest squeezed. If dad were here, he'd be relishing every moment of his first grandson.

I couldn't think of a better way to carry on his legacy than bring his traditions to my nephew's life. "I need to tell you about your grandpa." I warmed the bottle to the perfect temperature. "The guy was fearless."

I carried the little one back into the living room with the warm bottle in hand and tickled his lower lip with the nipple. He attacked it like he was starving, then stared at me with bright-blue eyes while he gulped the goodness down.

"He was a good man. He taught us to protect others and love the people we have while we have them. Family is everything." I swallowed hard as I stared down into Kip's eyes. "He'd have loved you."

My dad might not be here anymore, but I'd make up for his absence as best I could. I'd never fill the hole in this little's one's life as he would have, but I'd do my darnedest to be the best uncle I could be. It was an excellent way to honor my father.

CHAPTER THIRTEEN

MIRANDA

I stood outside Bayden's door, wondering what the heck I was doing. I'd handled the issue at work and was off for the rest of the evening. Instead of being smart, going home, and reminding myself of all the ways Bayden was wrong for me, I found myself on his front step like an idiot.

My heart kept speaking louder than my head. *What if we could be happy together?* He made me smile, and he brought out a playful side to me that has been missing since my sister. His presence made me feel safer than any other human being ever had. I didn't *need* him to keep me safe by any means but knowing he had my back meant the world.

I didn't let anyone in long enough to build trust, but something told me I could count on him. He was the first person I told about my sleepwalking episodes and the first person I allowed in my bed. He was someone I knew I could call and count on no matter what. I wanted him in my life, and I needed to figure out how to make it work.

If that meant talking to him honestly about how I feel about kids, then so be it. We'd have a serious, uncomfortable discussion. I didn't think I could delve into my past with him or anyone, but he said he could wait until I was ready to talk, and I knew he meant those words.

Still, his door seemed so imposing as I stood there, deciding if I should knock. Could I handle this conversation? Maybe waiting was a better idea. Or perhaps I needed to stop putting it off and give him the respect he deserved. He needed to know the truth or as much of it as I could tell him.

Before I could change my mind and turn back, I lifted my hand and rapped on the door with the back of my knuckles. The sound echoed, and he opened the door almost instantly. I peered up at him, surprised he'd gotten there so quickly.

"Were you standing right there?" I asked as the corners of my mouth tugged back into a smile

He shook his head, motioning me to be quiet with a single finger across his full, luscious lips. I wanted to kiss him more than anything and throw myself into his arms, but something in his motions and actions sent warning bells ringing in my mind. Swinging the door open, he gestured for me to come inside.

On edge, I approached the same way I did when I came upon an accident or robbery and wasn't sure what I'd find. All my senses went on alert, and my body tingled with the energy I'd need to fight or take flight.

Despite his odd behavior, there was no sign of tension in his shoulders, no worry tightening his features, no indication that something was wrong.

I reached out and touched him. "What's going on?" I didn't like the knotting dread in my gut.

He didn't answer but motioned for me to follow. I fell into step beside him, every nerve ending in my body firing off and lighting up. A chill skittered up my spine, and heat surged through my veins.

In the living room, a car seat sat next to the couch on the floor. Inside, a peacefully sleeping baby slumbered, and every muscle in my body locked up tight.

Bayden walked right up and scooped the tiny child up, his face lit with joy and love. With the baby cradled to his chest, he moved toward me.

I wanted to run, but I stood there, unable to breathe. A wave of terror flowed over me like a tsunami, followed by stinging prickles dancing across my skin. Beads of sweat pearled on my brow, and I swallowed a mouthful of bile as I stared at the baby in his arms.

He beamed at me, then back down at the baby.

"It's Kip," he said proudly. "I've got babysitting duty."

All my hopes of talking to him and discussing potential issues like this were dashed, as he smiled down at his nephew.

"Isn't he adorable?" Bayden beamed at me, and I offered a weak smile. I didn't know what to say, even if I could. Instead, I struggled to stay calm and not be uncomfortable as he talked.

"He sleeps so dang much. I've been telling him all about his grandfather, and how we're going to have a great time. I'm going to pass on all the things my dad taught me." The raw pain in his voice stirred me, but I couldn't pull out of my distress enough to reassure him.

His gaze met mine, and for the first time since he picked up the baby, he seemed to see me. "Are you okay?"

I nodded, swallowing hard.

"You don't look okay." He lowered the baby to the car seat, and the little one squirmed before settling into sleep once again. With that, Bayden walked up to me and wrapped me in a hug.

"You know, I don't think you're any less tough because you're afraid of babies." His warm tone tried to take some sting out of his words. I stared past him at the car seat, struggling against my past, and the overwhelming pain filling my chest—the thought of my mother's hateful words flooding my head.

The only experience I had with kids was my little sister. Given how that turned out, I wanted nothing to do with this baby. A nagging pain thundered in my temples, and I backed up out of his arms. As the baby squirmed and woke up, I watched.

His little pink face turned red as his mouth opened, and he let out a sound that could summon the devil himself. Terrified and unsure what to do, I took another step back as Bayden spoke softly to Kip.

"What's this all about?" He asked as the baby took another deep breath and screamed so hard, and so long, his little chin quivered. Bayden scooped the baby up and held him to his chest, gently massaging a circle between the child's shoulder blades. "It's probably gas," Bayden said to me.

I swallowed hard and took another step back. This wasn't for me. If I'd have known he had the baby, I never would have come here.

"What's with you and babies?" he asked, his gaze meeting mine as Kip settled down.

I shook my head.

"You can't shake your head. Clearly, there's *something*." He smiled at me as the baby let out an enormous burp.

I watched him rock the tiny infant back and forth. "He can't hurt you. You don't have to hold him or anything. I won't force him on you, but I want to know what's up. I want to understand you." His gentle tone and kind eyes eased some of the tension binding up my shoulders so tightly my neck and head ached.

My eyes filled with tears. How could I explain this deep-seated dislike of kids? How could I explain that I'm not cut out to be a mom? I mean, society had me on some clock like I'm only worthy if I procreate, but I don't subscribe to that kind of thinking. Trying to explain all of that wasn't easy because people judge or tell me I'll change my mind.

To top it all off, Bayden saw me as a protector; what would happen when he found out that the one child I had to protect died in my care? Would he take my side or my parents'?

He took a step toward me, and I backed up two steps.

"I know something is bothering you, but I am glad you came to see me." His words eased more of the cables squeezing my heart. "Was there something we needed to talk about?"

As he sat down on the couch, I recognized he was trying to make himself less imposing. He wanted to look at home, so I'd feel at home. It was a great technique—one I'd used to help people relax—but it only left me more on edge because I knew what he was doing.

He patted the couch beside him. "Want to sit with me?" His hopeful expression made me feel worse.

"Do you want kids of your own?" I blurted. I needed to know, even though I was sure I already knew the answer. He seemed so happy and at ease with the baby to not want a brood of his own.

"Well, maybe someday." He seemed taken aback by my question.

Just knowing he was open to the possibility of children while I was completely closed to the idea proved I needed to do the right thing and walk away.

Clammy with cold sweats, I inhaled. Letting the breath out slowly, I steeled myself against the awful truth. It didn't matter that Bayden made me happier than I had ever been because he made me feel whole and unbroken. He could give me everything I didn't know I needed, but none of that made a difference because I'd never be able to do the same for him, and he deserved better.

"Miranda?" His concerned expression left me aching. I glanced from him to the baby in his arms and struggled to process what to do next. What was there left to do? What was left to say?

I wanted to run out of his house and never come back, but something rooted me in place as he stood and moved toward me. The closer he came with the baby, the more nervous I got, and the more my heart thundered in my chest.

Escape. I needed to escape.

"Want to talk about whatever's going on?"

I shook my head, unable to process the moment as memories sprang up in my mind's eye. My sister's expression. The joy that turned to terror in a heartbeat. My feelings of helplessness.

"I'm right here if you need me." He took another step closer.

But I couldn't. I couldn't stay, couldn't let Bayden get closer. I needed to get out *now*. Without a word, I bolted for the front door.

CHAPTER FOURTEEN

BAYDEN

Friday morning dawned bright and early with Kip grumbling and warning me I better feed him soon. I smiled and hopped out of bed. It had been a busy night with the baby wanting food every three hours or so, but I didn't mind the broken sleep.

It gave me more time in the wee hours of the night to think about Miranda's sudden departure. As much as I wanted to follow her and figure out what the heck had gone wrong, I wasn't going to chase her with the baby in tow, and I wasn't sure hunting her down was the best option, anyway.

"I'll get your breakfast started," I said over my shoulder before leaving the room. My brother had brought over a little basket looking thing for the baby to sleep in, and I'd put it next to my bed.

Heading into the kitchen to heat some milk, I rubbed the grit out of my eyes and fired up my coffee maker. I could understand why they were so tired. Night after night of broken sleep had to take a toll on my brother and Kandra. One night was no big deal, but weeks? That had to be rough.

My thoughts drifted back to the sheer terror in Miranda's eyes when I'd approached her with Kip in my arms. I wasn't sure if she didn't like babies and didn't want to tell me that or if there was more to it. Maybe she was afraid of babies, but why?

I checked the milk to make sure it wasn't too hot as Kip's angry wail resounded through my home. "I'm on my way!" Carrying the bottle into my room, I scooped up the agitated baby and offered him the bottle.

He took it, suckling like he hadn't eaten for days even though it had only been—I checked my phone—less than three hours since I fed him last. He choked, and I sat him upright, taking the bottle so he could clear his airways.

His little face scrunched up, and I let him have the bottle back when I was sure he was done coughing.

Miranda asked if I wanted to have kids. Would my desire to be a father be a deal-breaker for her? Had I answered wrong? If I had, how could I fix it? I mean, I wouldn't mind children of my own, but they were not a requirement. With the right person, I'd be happy with just their company. I could have that familial fulfillment with my nephew or any other nieces or nephews my brothers might have.

Hell, I could join an organization to mentor youths and have that same sense of contentment. I didn't have to have my own.

I sighed as Kip gulped milk, hardly bothering to take breaths in between. "Nothing is ever easy, is it?" I asked him.

He glanced at me, then focused on his food again. My phone rang, and I answered it, hoping Miranda would be on the other end.

"Good morning. How goes it?" Kandra's cheerful voice met my ear, and I smiled.

"It goes well. Kip is having breakfast. When he's finished, I'll bring him home. I bet you're missing him."

She laughed. "You know, we really are. Maybe we're crazy. A good night's sleep is fantastic, but I just miss him so much."

"I get it, I do. I'm happy to do this again whenever you're ready." I meant it.

"We appreciate it." Her warm voice brought a smile to my lips. "See you in a few and thank you again."

"It was my pleasure." We got off the phone, and I admired the sleeping bundle in my arms. "Your parents miss you, and I'm going to miss you when you go home."

I LOWERED the diaper bag to the floor and offered Kandra the car seat. "Here he is, happy and healthy like I promised."

She wrapped an arm around my shoulder and gave me a quick hug before taking the sleeping baby. As she walked off with him, I unpacked the leftover milk and put it in the fridge.

"You can leave it," Noah said, sneaking up on me and giving me a bear hug. "Thank you, brother."

"Anytime." I offered him the bag, and he took it. As he unpacked the empty bottles, he put them in a sink full of suds. I added a bottle brush to my must-haves list at home so I could bring them clean bottles the next time. Tired parents didn't need to be doing more dishes. "The bassinet is in my back seat. Want me to grab it?"

"I'll get it in a minute. I jump at any excuse for fresh air and a stretch." He chuckled, scrubbing the bottles with hot soapy water.

I went in search of Kandra and found her holding Kip in the living room.

"Can I talk to you for a second?" I asked.

"Sure." She smiled, rocking Kip back and forth.

"I don't think Miranda likes babies." The words sounded strange out there in the open like that, and she studied me for a second as if unsure I said what she thought she heard.

"Why do you think she doesn't like babies?" Kandra's expression shifted to confusion as she turned her weight to one hip and cradled Kip in her arms.

I sighed and sat down on the couch. "She came over last night."

A slight smile curved the corners of her lips.

"It's not like that," I said. "She looked like she was going to have a panic attack over Kip. She wouldn't let me get close to her with him

and wouldn't come close to me while I held him. She refused to stay."
The whole bizarre event still bothered me as I thought about everything that happened.

"Did she say anything?"

"She asked if I wanted kids."

Kandra's lips formed a perfect 'o' of surprise. "You're serious,
then?"

Her teasing tone brought a smile to my lips.

"I think she was testing me. Like she has a list of absolutes, and
one of them is no kids." I hoped the words would sound ridiculous,
but they made far too much sense.

Kandra sat down next to me. "That's rough. Have you prepared
for that possibility? What about you?"

I nodded. "I mean, I think I want children, but it's not a relationship ender for me. I mean, I'm happy playing uncle." I meant the
words, and Kandra nodded.

"Having kids is a lot of work." Her tired sigh and the night I spent
with the baby backed up her claim. "I think you need to make sure
you're okay with the possibility of not having kids of your own. Especially if she has that negative of a reaction to them. Make sure it is not
something you'll regret later and then talk to her about it."

She was making sense. "You're right. I should talk to myself
before I talk to her. It's important to have the facts straight in my head
before I lay them out and build a future off of them."

"Are you two serious? I mean talking babies serious?" she gave me
a sideways glance.

"You're not giving up, are you?"

She lifted her shoulders. "You don't have to answer; I know the
truth. You Lockharts are all in when it comes to love. I'm glad she
makes you happy. You both deserve that."

I agreed, but I couldn't help but wonder if she was right. Would I
decide kids are not a deal-breaker, then regret it later in life? Would it
eventually drive a wedge between Miranda and me? I didn't think it
would, but I was wise enough to know that things could change. Our

perspectives shift every year we're alive. We're continually growing, and locking myself into a child-free relationship might very well be something that bothered me down the line.

"You better not be putting moves on my wife." Noah walked through the door with the bassinet in hand. He moved toward their bedroom, and Kandra laughed.

"Oh, honey, he has his own woman issues." Even though she was talking to his retreating back, I felt the humor radiating off of him.

"Don't give her a reason to leave you. We both know I'm the better-looking brother," I said to Noah's back with a laugh, and Kandra rolled her eyes at both of us.

Noah walked back into the room a moment later and rubbed his hands together. "Woman issues, huh?" He glanced at me, then at Kandra. "Does this have anything to do with you spending a lot more time with a certain sheriff we all know and love?"

Despite his slightly gleeful expression, Kandra gave a warning shake of her head.

"She doesn't want kids," I said.

Noah seemed stunned, all the humor vanishing from his face in an instant and a severe expression taking over. "How do you know?"

"She asked if I wanted kids, then bolted after refusing to get anywhere near Kip." I figured I might as well be honest with him. I rarely opened up to my brother about relationships, but it was nice to know I could talk to him when I needed to.

"She was at your place?" His eyes widened, which told me exactly what he was thinking.

"She stopped by for a minute and didn't stay long when she found out the baby was there. I think she wanted to talk about something." Talking about the odd interaction helped me realize there might be more to the whole situation than I first thought.

"Sure, *talk* about something." Noah's joking tone earned him a kick from Kandra.

"You're focused on the wrong part," she told him.

He rubbed his leg with a hangdog expression on his face. "I'm poking fun, sheesh." He glanced at me. "What are you going to do now?"

I needed to decide if kids were a must-have for me. Maybe it wasn't a deal-breaker now, but I needed to put some thought into my future, too. Still, the more I considered it, the more confident I was that it was no contest. I wanted Miranda. Yes, maybe kids would enrich that life, but none of the rest of it mattered without her.

"I'm going to think about it to be sure, and then I'll talk to her." Uneasy for a second, I wondered if she'd even be willing to talk. Last night, as the door closed behind her, I had a sinking feeling that things were over between us, though no such thing had been said.

"I'm sorry." My brother lifted and gave me a quick hug. "Relationships are hard."

I nodded, knowing he understood more than most people. He and Kandra's relationship had been stormy too. Heck, theirs had been downright tumultuous, but they made it through because they loved one another.

If I loved Miranda, we'd figure this out.

The L-word, really?

I hadn't said it or even thought about it before, but the more I considered my hopes and dreams for a future with her, the more that word made sense. I wouldn't tell anyone else this, but it added another layer of uncertainty and difficulty to the existing strain on our potential relationship.

"Thank you, both of you," I said.

Kandra nodded, and my brother stared at the floor. Kip made little noises, and Kandra rocked him before Noah took him from her.

"I'm going to head out. Let me know next time you want me to watch him." I left, thinking about Miranda the entire way home.

CHAPTER FIFTEEN

MIRANDA

My phone rang, and I stared at the TV, not hearing a word or seeing the show I'd put on. Honestly, I didn't know what was playing but used the background noise as a distraction. It wasn't working.

Jolted out of my thoughts, I glanced at the phone on the coffee table. Was it my mother calling? Did I dare check? After four rings, the call went to voicemail, and I exhaled. What if it was Bayden?

The thought made me feel bad, both for missing the call and not having the energy, or maybe it was courage, to call him back.

A knock at the door sent my heart into overdrive. I knew Bayden was at the door.

Could I even face him?

He knocked again, and I stood up, slogging my way to the door. Gathering my courage, I unlocked the deadbolts and opened it two inches to peek at him through the crack.

Bayden's warm expression did something to my insides, and the smell of garlic and pizza hit me full force. My stomach growled, and I thought back to if I'd eaten anything all day. I couldn't remember.

"I can leave the food," he said, offering the white pizza box and the Styrofoam container on top.

I shook my head and opened the door wide. I needed him and threw myself into his arms, so relieved he was here on my step and bearing gifts of food.

"I'm glad you're here," I said honestly, blinking back unexpected tears. I was ashamed of how I handled everything, but I didn't know how to do better.

"I'm glad to be here." He looked past me to my phone sitting on the table. "I tried to call."

My shoulders dropped a bit. "Sorry I didn't answer. I'm kind of avoiding my phone right now." Honesty felt good, even if I wasn't comfortable giving him more than that.

He nodded. "I have those days too."

I let him in and closed the door behind us. "Is this a date?" I asked, dangling a single shred of playfulness before him like a string before a cat.

He grinned. "Is it?"

"I think so," I said. I needed this moment of normalcy. My life lacked stability, support, and ordinary moments like these. Despite our inability to be serious—and my guilt over that—I wanted to enjoy this.

He put the food on the coffee table and turned to me, his lips curving at the edges. Having him here helped me breathe a little easier. The smell of pizza and garlic knots had my mouth watering and my stomach begging for sustenance.

"Let's sit and relax," I said, plopping on the couch.

He sat. His tight expression left me feeling that he wanted to ask questions, but he stayed quiet and opened the clamshell container in front of him, revealing garlic knots. "I wasn't sure what you'd want."

I shrugged. "I'm easy." The second I said the words, a grin crossed my lips at my unintended double meaning.

He chuckled before opening the pizza. Inside was Roy's special everything pizza loaded with meats and veggies.

It was my favorite, but there was no way Bayden knew that. We'd never talked about food. Then again, I wouldn't put it past him to ask

Roy, as he'd done with my coffee. He always showed he cared in so many ways.

I wanted to tell him everything, but I wasn't sure I could. Still, I needed to say something to explain my behavior. "Look, I wanted to talk—"

He held up a hand and fixed me with a serious expression. "Before you start, I want to tell you that you don't owe me any explanations. I'm honestly happy to be here spending time with you."

My heart squeezed, and I stared at him, lost for words. Swallowing hard, I nodded. "Thank you." Knowing he felt the same way I did—that spending time together was amazing—helped put me at ease, but also made me ache more.

I knew we needed to talk. Before either of us got in any deeper, he needed to know my stance on kids because it had the potential to change or end our whole budding relationship.

"Did you ask Roy what my favorite pizza was?" I probed, giving him a suspicious, playful glare.

He shook his head. "This is my favorite, so I hoped you'd like it too." His grin made my chest feel full, and I struggled to inhale.

"I hate it." I couldn't hold back a grin as his expression fell. "Just kidding, it's my favorite too."

"You're messing with me." The roll of his eyes earned a shake of my head. "No way my favorite pizza is your favorite too."

"It is my favorite pizza. No joke." I grabbed a piece and dug in. He laughed and followed suit. The hot deliciousness had my stomach growling, and a mushroom slipped off the side of the slice and dangled by a dangerously thin piece of cheese.

"Careful." He pointed, and I grabbed the escaping mushroom between my thumb and index finger before putting it back on the slice.

When I took a bite, I eyed the pizza for a second. "Roy makes the best pizza around." He had no way of knowing how badly I needed this ordinary, calm moment after the stress of this time of year and my interactions with my mother.

Bayden was the closest thing I'd had to a friend since ... well ... ever. My past, my family, and my struggles didn't afford luxuries like friends. Hell, it was those issues that made me a rotten friend. As Bayden was learning, I could never open up to anyone. Friends weren't supposed to keep each other at arm's length, but for me, I would have to keep them at a full body's length to spare them the hurt and shame I felt.

It was simpler to keep people away and out of my life, except in the most superficial ways.

"Garlic knots too." Bayden snagged one and popped it into his mouth.

"I asked him when he's going to fill the knots with cheese, and he said he'll try to make that work." I took another bite of my pizza while Bayden gave me a look like I'd told him the sexiest secret.

While we ate, we discussed toppings and other easy, fluffy topics. He made me forget my stress for a moment. The conversation shifted to curiosity about how people could choose low-carb diets. I laughed when he almost dropped his pizza, and he threw a bit of bread at me.

For a moment, we were like any other typical couple enjoying their time together.

But I did what I do and screwed it up. "You need to stop showing up here when I'm not taking texts or calls."

He froze.

My heart sank to my feet, and that little voice in my head shouted, *what are you doing?*

What was I doing? I was keeping him at a distance and pushing him away because I'm a terrible friend.

He swallowed his bite. "Okay. Sorry for showing up without being invited." He casually studied his pizza as if worried about the structural integrity of the slice. "I thought we were beyond the formalities. I mean ... *you* showed up at my house."

For some reason, his response sucked the tension out of the moment, and everything smoothed over. Instead, the feeling that I could be honest filled me, and I went with it. "I did, and you're right, but sometimes I need my space, and I need you to respect that."

He nodded calmly. "Okay. I'll work on being better about that. Can we work something out, so if I'm worried, you respond in some way, shape, or form? I need to know you're not dead and haven't sleepwalked into traffic or something?"

That made me pause. I never even considered Bayden might worry like that. "Sure. How about an all-safe word? If I text that, you know I'm okay."

"Perfect. What's the word?" he studied me, his slice of pizza seemingly forgotten in his hand.

"Let's keep it simple. *Safe.*" No matter how broken-down I might feel, I could manage a four-letter text to him, right?

"Easy. I like it. Now, would you like me to leave?"

I shook my head. "No! Please stay..." I said.

My heart was begging me to let him stay, but my brain knew better. The more time we spent together, the harder it would be to let him go.

Needing to cover for my overzealous response, I cleared my throat and calmly said, "You're here, and I'm enjoying your company." The constriction of my chest eased with the words, and I changed the topic. "It must have been hard to pick pizza toppings with such a large family."

He grinned. "Nah, we had a system. My dad was wonderful at keeping the peace, and my mom was a trooper. She was kind and loving, but firm when we needed it." His eyes misted over. "They were a team, and they did a good job with us. I think."

I could agree with that.

"I love that you and your family are so close." How many families did I know where the brother and sister-in-law could ask another brother to watch the baby? None. Then again, I didn't know a lot of families because I kept my distance from everyone.

"Me too. We're certainly lucky." He took another bite of his pizza, chewing thoughtfully. After he swallowed, he glanced at me. "What about you? What's your family like?"

An arctic chill bolted through me like I'd been speared with an icicle. I thought about my mother. My father. My family. "We ... aren't close—never were." That was putting it mildly, but I was proud I said anything at all. My family had always been an off-limits topic I didn't discuss with anyone.

"I'm sorry." He reached out and touched my hand, and I stared at the tingling contact.

"Me too." I wished for a large, close family, but that wasn't in the cards for me. Finishing my slice, I tried not to focus on what I wished my life had been instead of what it was. "Thank you for the pizza." I inhaled and settled back on the couch.

Bayden looked at the box, then at me. "You're not done, are you? We have a whole pizza to eat, and you're not pulling your weight here."

His incredulous glance made me laugh harder, and I couldn't help but lean in and press my lips to his. It was too perfect a moment not to enjoy him a little more.

The tangy taste of the red sauce on his lips didn't scare me away, and I wanted to deepen the kiss despite the warning bells clanging in my head. I backed off and noticed his suspicious stare.

"What was that for?"

I lifted both shoulders. "Had to shut you up somehow," I joked.

"Did you just..." he couldn't finish his sentence through his faux outrage. I was content with life for the moment but wished for a future with the man beside me.

"Tell me more about your family. Where did you grow up?"

His innocent question put my guard up instantly. "It was me and my mom and dad. As I said, we're not close." There wasn't much more I wanted to share.

He seemed surprised. "Is there a reason you're not close?"

I shook my head. "We just aren't." I don't think my parents

wanted kids. I think I was a mistake, and my sister was the saving grace. I blinked back tears and sighed.

"I'm sorry." He pulled me in for a hug before changing the subject back to my lightweight pizza status.

"I've seen you put back as many beers as any of the guys, and you're telling me one slice will do you?" The laughter in his eyes brought mine back.

"What can I say? I'm a cheap date if you're feeding me pizza instead of buying me beer."

He pointed to the box. "We're going to work on that."

CHAPTER SIXTEEN

BAYDEN

"Did you invite her?" My mother studied me as I set the table for our usual Sunday dinner. She had asked me to invite Miranda, and I did, but Miranda politely declined. I knew there were issues with her family—she said as much—but I didn't understand why she'd be hesitant to spend time with mine. I knew they'd accept her as one of their own.

"Yes. She said thank you for the kind offer, but she's unable to join us." I couldn't stop thinking about how much fun we had yesterday, talking, laughing, eating pizza, and enjoying one another's company.

"We don't bite." Ethan bumped his shoulder into me as he walked by.

"He doesn't speak for me," Quinn said as he headed into the kitchen to keep working on the food.

I glanced at my mother, lifting a helpless shoulder as she smiled and shook her head at my brother's antics.

"I'm sorry she said no. Maybe next time." Her hopeful tone saddened me. I doubted Miranda was going to come around by next

Saturday, and I didn't blame her. Whatever had happened in her past traumatized her.

Her family relationship was in shambles, and I'd never seen someone as sad as she'd been while telling me they were never close. It was apparent there was more to it than she was willing to share.

As much as I wanted to break down her walls and get to the heart of her suffering, I knew that wasn't the way to help her. I promised myself that I'd become the shoulder she leaned on when she needed one.

"Pretty sure your food is burning." Quinn almost made me drop the fork in my hand until I remembered I had prepared a salad, and he was messing with me.

"Pretty sure, no one thinks you're funny."

He snorted. "I think I'm funny." With that, he disappeared into the kitchen as my mother fixed me with a look I didn't like. I quickly placed the last fork and headed for the kitchen to grab the salad I'd thrown together.

My brothers brought out their dishes, but I barely noticed as the image of Miranda pinching an escaping mushroom and dropping it right back on her slice filled my mind. Her smile replayed in my head, and laughter hung in my ears.

"When's the wedding?" Noah elbowed me, and Kandra flashed me an apologetic grin as we took our seats around the table.

"What wedding? Thought you made an honest woman out of her already." I stared at Noah, silently warning him to keep his mouth shut.

He chuckled, and my brothers all shifted in their seats. Ethan checked his phone and earned a sharp sound of disapproval from our mother. He quickly put it away, and Quinn glanced from me to Noah, his brows pitched high on his forehead.

"Let's eat." My mother inhaled deeply. "Everything looks and smells so good."

Conversations started up around the table, but I was stuck in my head again, thinking about the sorrow in Miranda's eyes. I couldn't imagine growing up without this support system. Sure, we didn't always get along, but we were still there for one another.

The baby started crying, and I gestured at Noah and Kandra to enjoy their meal while standing up.

"He might be gassy." Kandra smiled her thanks.

I scooped up Kip and rocked him gently before placing him on my shoulder. Rubbing gentle circles between his shoulder blades, I moved slowly, ignoring everyone else but the little man in my arms. He blinked at me, gave a toothless, old-man grin, then let out a huge belch.

"That's gotta feel better," I said, continuing to rock him.

"Who knew Bayden would be good with babies?" Quinn said to Ethan, who was busy looking at his phone under the table.

"Who knew Bayden would be good at anything?" Ethan said, then glanced up and around the table as if he couldn't believe he'd said that out loud. I knew he said it in good humor, but I couldn't help but wonder if there was a serious undertone there. Ethan and my relationship had shifted over the last few months, and I knew why.

"When are you and Miranda going to get together and have kids?" Quinn's question earned him a glare from both Noah and Kandra, and I knew my brother and sister-in-law were trying to stare my other brother into silence.

He shrugged at them and glowered at me, empty fork in hand.

Kip yawned, and I lowered him back into his swing and buckled him up before returning to my spot at the table without saying a word. What could I say? I wasn't about to out Miranda for not wanting kids. I already felt bad enough that I talked to Noah and Kandra about it. After all, that was Miranda's secret, and I had no right to share her personal information with anyone. I'd made peace with my need for backup and support, but I didn't feel good about potentially betraying her trust.

"When are you going to mind your own damn business?" I asked Quinn before looking directly at Ethan. "How is Angie?"

He jerked his head up and glared at me. "How the hell would I know?"

"Oh, my mistake, I guess." My attempt to throw my family off my scent seemed to work as all heads swiveled toward Ethan, curious about this tidbit.

"Maybe we should ask *you* how she is?" Ethan's lip curled into a slight sneer as he narrowed his eyes at me.

"Sheesh, you sound jealous, brother. I'm not interested in Angie. Not one bit." I took a drink of my water as the air in the room thickened like Mom's gravy.

"Stop it, you two." Mom turned to Kandra and asked questions about Kip, but Ethan didn't stop glaring at me. Quinn didn't stop glancing from one to the other of us, and Noah's worried expression told me he was putting everything together. *Finally.*

All I cared about was that no one was grilling me about Miranda anymore.

I pulled out my phone, comfortable that Mom was busy talking to Kandra, and sent Miranda a text. *Thinking about you.*

Knowing she was aching killed me. I couldn't get the thought of her telling me to stop showing up at her place out of my head. I honestly thought we were past the formalities with the time we shared, but I'd gravely miscalculated.

I told myself I'd do better with no more unannounced, uninvited visits. I'd respect her boundaries and wishes, but I didn't like the thought of her sitting at home, alone, without family to lean on.

My brothers might drive me insane, but I could count on them, and they could count on me. We'd gotten each other through some tough times.

"Are you eating that or making love to it?" Ethan scowled at me from across the table as I stared at the lettuce on my fork.

"If you think looking at something is the same as making love to it,

I have some news about why you're single." I popped the bite into my mouth and crunched down as Quinn laughed out loud. I studied Ethan, daring him to say something else. I wasn't putting up with anyone's garbage tonight. Every comment would go for the throat if he wanted to mess with me.

"Do I need to separate you two?" My mother's tone told me she was done with our shenanigans, though I heard the warmth and love underneath. She knew we'd work through our issues like we always had.

Ethan took a drink of his water, his dirty look not easing up one bit.

Even with him mad at me, I was grateful for my family. I knew this was a bump in the road; it wasn't serious, and the feud wouldn't last. How must Miranda feel? Helpless and hopeless to fix her situation? I couldn't imagine that she wouldn't have made every attempt to repair whatever had happened between them.

At least, a lot more made sense now. I could understand her private nature and her closed-off attitude. Getting any details from her was like trying to get water from a stone. She was holding back because of pain, possibly shame, maybe even fear. Whatever her past was, it was terrible.

"This is great," I said to Quinn as I took a bite of the thick stew he made.

"Thanks. I'll give you the recipe." He finished his last bite, his worried gaze still darting from me to Ethan.

Mom and Kandra got back to talking in a low voice, and I glanced at baby Kip, who was chewing on his foot and smiling at the ceiling as the swing rocked him gently. I glanced at the picture of my father watching over us and wondered what he'd say if he were here with us now.

He'd be disappointed in mine and Ethan's tiff, but he understood boys. I didn't doubt for a second he'd be holding Kip and never putting him down. He'd be telling him stories he told us a million times.

I'd give anything to hear one of his stories again or have him sitting right there in his empty chair, watching us talk, smiling happily as his eyes gave away how proud he was of all of us.

I was grateful for his lessons and my family's love. For all the crucial moments, I'd been able to turn to them, and the times of need when they turned to me.

"So, Quinn, have you met anyone yet?" Noah's voice broke into my reverie. I glanced at my brother, curiously. Did Noah know something about my twin that I didn't?

Quinn shook his head, and I had a sense he was telling the truth. "Nah, I'm busy building my career, unlike all you chumps."

I chuckled. It's not like we didn't all put in our fair share of hours into the family business. We were nearing the end of the new Sheriff Headquarters project, and all our hard work was showing.

I checked my phone under the table, hoping for a message from Miranda, but there was nothing. Maybe it was time to revisit the old farm, and not because I felt closer to Dad out there.

I finished the last bite of my dinner. My brothers had outdone themselves with Quinn's hearty stew, the delicious homemade cheddar bacon biscuits Noah made from scratch, and Ethan's fruit salad. Everything had been delicious.

Kandra laughed at something Mom said, and I glanced at them. Kip heard his mother and began looking for her past them, and I smiled at the curious look on his round little face.

Noah asked Ethan why he'd missed the after-work drinks yesterday, and I opened my ears for my brother's answer, but Ethan had nothing to say. Quinn volunteered that Ethan had been strangely busy lately, and Noah agreed.

I took a drink of my water and studied Ethan's face. His frown made me wonder what he'd been up to. I assumed I'd known, but I wasn't so sure.

In my lap, my phone lit up, and my heart leaped. Maybe instead of going out to the farm tonight, I would get to see Miranda the old-fashioned way, without risk of arrest. I didn't mind the change of plans. Especially when the plans potentially involved the woman I was sure I was falling for. I quickly checked the message, but my heart sank when I saw it wasn't from Miranda at all.

The text was from Angie.

Without even opening it, I glanced at Ethan.

CHAPTER SEVENTEEN

MIRANDA

"When are you coming home?" My mother's screech filled my ears, and I squeezed my eyes closed, wishing this nightmare was over. Thoughts of Bayden came to mind. His gentle hugs, his kindness, the warmth in his smile, and I clung to that for comfort.

"I'm not coming back." I could hardly speak around the lump in my throat.

Her voice rose to that pitch that usually set off neighborhood dogs. "Good! We don't want you to come back. We'd lock the doors and call the cops on you like the criminal you are."

I put my back to the darkest corner of my closet and slid down. Drawing my legs to my chest, I planted my chin on my knees and struggled not to let her words cut me. I wanted to tell her I wasn't a criminal. I was one of the good guys, but I knew that all logic was lost while she was in the middle of an episode.

She needed to vent. It was healthy for her to get the words off her chest. She needed this outlet. A hundred times I promised myself that I'd change my number, but I couldn't bring myself to do it. What if something terrible happened and they couldn't reach me? This was my penance, and I'd resigned myself to take the abuse years ago.

Why didn't it ever get easier? Each hysterical call felt like every bone in my body was breaking. Why did her calls reduce me to nothing?

"Are you listening to me?" The words pierced through my skull like nails from a nail gun, and I blinked back tears.

"I'm listening." It was hard not to when she was screaming.

"You know it's all your fault. All of it. You let it happen!" The frenzied edge of her voice made me wince, and I struggled to bring my heart rate back to a reasonable level.

I was trying to be a dutiful daughter by letting her work through her grief like this. I wanted her to find peace, but she'd seemed to grow worse over the years, not better, and it killed me.

"I'm sorry." I was sorry for everything that had happened. I was sad for all the pain we'd suffered. I hated the rift between us. I wanted a family like Bayden's. I could have enjoyed family dinners, after-work drinks, and a business run by the tight-knit group.

"You're not sorry! You've never been sorry!" The crash of broken glass on the other end of the line warned me she'd smashed something, and I held back a sigh.

"Is Dad there?" Was she safe, at least? Was someone watching over her to make sure she didn't hurt herself?

"What do you care?" The piercing sound of her voice slipped deftly between my ribs like a knife to puncture my heart. "She's asking about you."

In the background, my dad growled something I couldn't make out. At least she wasn't alone.

"He said it's none of your damn business if he's here." Her fury boiled over. "Why? Are you done talking to me? Done listening to the truth? Are you going to admit what you did?"

I shook my head, tears rolling down my cheeks. I wanted normalcy and stability and for my mother and father not to hate me so much. I needed them not to blame me for everything because they were wrong; it wasn't my fault, but year after year, I heard the same story, and it always ended the same: yelling, accusations, and tears.

We'd hang up, and the cycle would repeat until the day she would finally wear herself out.

I was tired of it all—tired of the same awful feelings and painful conversations. Done with the animosity and vile she spewed every time we talked.

I should have expected her call and knew they'd get more frequent; they always did this time of year. It was nearing the anniversary of that awful day.

"Did you hang up on me?" Another crash of glass followed her rage.

"I'm still here." I could only whisper the words as tears streamed down my cheeks.

"Well? Are you going to admit what you did?" The other end of the line went so quiet I wondered if she was holding her breath.

I opened my mouth, but the pain welling up in me overflowed, and my voice broke. Unable to speak, I heard her scream again, but I was swept up in the tidal wave of pain and loss. Could I handle another year of this? Could I take another week of this? Could I handle the rest of this call? I wasn't sure anymore.

"I knew you wouldn't take responsibility." The caustic hatred in her voice burned like acid on raw skin, and I tried to shrug away the pain as I hid in the shadowy corner, safe only because the walls pressed against my back, and the darkness swallowed me whole.

Her only way to contact me was to call. She didn't know where I was because I didn't want her to find me. If she came here and ruined all the peace I'd worked so hard to create, I don't know what I'd do.

"You're not my daughter. I disown you." As venom spewed from her lips, I searched internally for a cure-all, but there wasn't one. I couldn't talk sanity into a crazy person.

No, I'd continue to answer because it was the least invasive. Giving up wasn't something my mother knew how to do. If I didn't answer, she'd find me, and that was a scenario I wasn't willing to consider.

"Your father wouldn't miss you either." She continued, showing no signs of stopping the tirade anytime soon, and I braced for impact.

I imagined Bayden's arms around me, holding me close and soothing away the hurt blistering through my being. I wanted nothing more than to be held by him during this painful and never-ending guilt trip.

"Are you ignoring me?"

"No." My whispered word ricocheted off the cave-like walls of the closet as if someone else was shouting it back at me.

"Then why aren't you speaking up?" Her tone rose another octave somehow, and I cringed.

"I didn't want to interrupt you." The second I said the words, I knew I shouldn't have. She inhaled, the sound as unsettling as tree branches squeaking against a window in the middle of the night.

"I—I need to go." I went to hang up as she started shouting, but something stopped me, and I stared at the phone a moment, able to hear every word of resentment pouring out of her mouth.

I slowly lifted the phone back to my ear. If I hung up, it would be worse. She'd call back, over and over, until she got to say all the things she wanted to tell me.

As she continued to attack me, I thought once more of Bayden and his warm lips on my forehead, whispering that everything would be all right. In my mind, he was right here beside me, helping me weather this storm.

I thought about his smile, and the pain ravishing my soul eased.

The line went dead in my ear, and I glanced at my phone. But there wasn't an ounce of light in the closet. My phone must have died. How long had I been sitting there, thinking of Bayden while my mother laid into me?

I shifted on my numb backside. Uneasy, the phone slipped through my hand. The soft thump of it hitting the floor was somehow comforting, and I hugged my legs in the dark. Blinking back the pain, I hated the tight feeling in my face. The dried tears coated my skin, and I wanted to scratch as a stray tear rolled down my cheek.

I needed to plug in my phone, but the edge of my bed seemed so far away. My charger cord might as well have been on another planet.

The need to call Bayden filled me, and I glanced where I thought my dead phone had fallen. Picking it up, I tried to turn it on. Holding the power button, I waited for it to power up to tell me I had three percent left, but the screen stayed black. No light filled the small space, and I sat there, thinking about how poetic it was that I was trapped in the dark and my only means of light was out of my reach.

I wanted Bayden's strength and his unending support. Even if I couldn't talk about what was going on, he'd understand. I craved that acceptance and his "no questions asked, no judgment passed" method of loving me.

Love?

I didn't think he loved me, did I? I mean, how could he? He knew nothing about me. I was acting like a silly, lovesick teenager. Yes, Bayden was a great guy, but love? It was too soon for that. Right?

I stared out the closet door toward the window, and a sliver of moonlight called to me. There was no way I'd call Bayden at such a late hour, anyway. A little voice in my mind whispered that maybe he'd show up unexpectedly.

The second that hopeful thought cropped up, I remembered how I told him off for inviting himself over. I made damn sure he'd never show up and catch me in a vulnerable moment again.

Even if he showed up, how would he get in? I locked the deadbolts. The house was dark. Bayden wouldn't break down the door to find me; he'd assume I was asleep like a normal human being and leave without disturbing me.

I was alone. Wholly, utterly, alone.

And for the first time, I didn't want to be alone with my pain and grief. I wanted to be with him.

I needed to be stronger, stand up, and go plug in my phone. I needed to be the badass woman I had to be and stop cowering in my closet.

Exhaustion swept through me. Would it be so bad to let someone help me through a challenging moment? Could I be a badass and also lean on someone sometimes?

Despite the questions, no answers presented themselves.

I couldn't muster an ounce of energy to get to my feet, much less walk to my bedside table. Instead, I put my forehead on my knees and cried until complete exhaustion consumed me.

CHAPTER EIGHTEEN

BAYDEN

I glanced at my phone. It was nearly one in the afternoon, and Miranda hadn't gotten back to me after last night's texts at dinner. I didn't want to keep messaging her because I wanted to respect what she said about needing her time alone.

Still, I hated not hearing from her, and she hadn't even sent the agreed-on word so I would know she was safe.

"Uh-oh, I know that look."

I turned my head toward the voice and saw Max in his navy shorts with his mailbag slung over his shoulder. His hair was black and silver at the temples, and his dark eyes were sparkling in the afternoon sunshine. I waved him over to the front patio and offered him a beer from my cooler.

He shook his head but sat beside me, running his hand over his close-clipped gray goatee as if to smooth it down. He said nothing, and my thoughts boiled over.

"I think I might love Miranda, but she has some issues that we need to work through." The words burst out, surprising me. I trusted Max and knew he wouldn't tell a soul about anything I confided in him.

"Everybody has issues." Max's thoughtful tone had me nodding. He was right, though I couldn't help but feel that Miranda and I might have a few more problems than the average couple. That is unless I thought about how rocky things had been between Noah and Kandra.

I fiddled with the icy beer, watching the beads of condensation roll down the outside of the bottle. "That's true, but how do you work through issues with someone who refuses to discuss them?" The lack of communication and the way she shut me out had been bothering me. How could we work on anything if she wasn't even willing to tell me there was a problem?

"You can't force someone to talk to you." Max smiled into the sunshine while squinting up into the blue sky. A few fluffy white clouds drifted past, and a stiff wind blew in off the creek. "Give her time. Either she'll come around, or she won't. Either way, you'll know."

I nodded. "I hope Miranda comes around. I care about her."

"I'm sure she knows that."

I looked at Max, but he was staring off into space while he continued talking. "Just keep being there for her when she needs you. Keep being her rock, and the rest will follow."

Taking a deep drink of my frosty beer, I watched some crows fly by. What Max said made sense, but I was kind of hoping for more that I could do on my end. "Is there anything I can do to help her talk to me?"

"Be someone she can trust. Give her space when she needs it and let her know she's in your thoughts." Max still seemed contemplative.

"Thank you for talking to me about this." I'd been struggling—and still was—but having someone to talk to had helped.

"No problem. I think it'll take time. Try to be patient. She'll open up when she's ready, and I'm sure you'll be able to work things out." Max lifted his shoulders and let them back down slowly.

I hoped he was right. "It's difficult because communication is so important to me." It had never been before, but I'd never been serious about anyone before. Miranda meant everything to me, so doing things right was necessary.

"Have you tried telling her that?" Max glanced at me, and I thought back.

I was sure I hadn't, but we weren't quite in an actual relationship. "It's... complicated," I said honestly. "We haven't made anything official. Do I have the right to make demands?"

"You're setting reasonable boundaries and making your needs known. There's nothing demanding about that." Max chuckled. "Even if it's not official, she needs to know what you're all about. Otherwise, how can she figure out if you're right for her?"

He had a very valid point, one I hadn't thought of before. I needed to have a candid conversation with her and let her know that I wanted things between us to be serious, but I would wait as long as necessary. Like Max pointed out, I had to make my intentions clear.

"You're in this for the long haul, then?" Max asked.

I waited for the fear that should have accompanied his words, but none came.

"I think so. I can see myself with her long term." Provided we could get the communication down. I loved the woman she was, her quirky humor, even her darker side. I didn't mind her sleep issues. I wanted to hold her tight and keep her safe. She had a troubled past, but we could work through that and whatever else she was dealing with.

"That's good. I think you and the sheriff fit well together." Max's grin stretched ear to ear. "You need to understand that things are always complicated. Don't get it in your head that you'll talk, and everything will suddenly be roses."

I nodded. I knew that, and I was prepared to face whatever issues came next. With her by my side, I knew we could get through almost anything. "I know. I do have a few other concerns, though. How do you know when something is a deal-breaker?"

Max stiffened up. "Well, that's different for everyone. Decide what's worth working through and what's not. Is there something specific you're thinking about? Or are you giving me a generality?"

There was something specific, but I wasn't sure it was my place to share her secret. I knew Max wouldn't say a word, but did I have the right to tell him?

"Scout's honor, what you say here stays here." Max lifted a hand as if swearing an oath.

"I know," I said with a nod, "I worry if talking about it is betraying her trust."

"Well, you don't have to talk about it if you'd rather not. I respect that you're concerned with how she might feel about you discussing her secrets. That goes a long way to telling me how you feel about her." Max's voice filled with pride.

"She seems to have an aversion to babies." I swallowed hard and stared at the nearly full beer in my hand. "I worry she's not going to want kids."

Max sucked a breath between his teeth, producing a hissing sound. "I see why you're asking about deal-breakers because that is a tough one."

We sat in silence, and I wiped the condensation from my drink on my jeans before setting the bottle down. I wasn't much of a day drinker—outside of our after-work drinks—and I could nurse a single beer for most of the day. It was more of a refreshment than anything.

"I mean, I'm not ready for kids right now." I loved my nephew, but I wasn't ready to take on that kind of thing full time. I'd stick with babysitting and enjoy all the best parts while knowing I got to send him home at the end of the day.

"I'm not sure anyone is ever ready for kids, even if they think they are, but I understand what you're saying." Max chuckled. "Did she tell you she's against having kids?"

"Well, no, but..." Why else would she run out like she had when I was watching Kip?

"So maybe talk to her instead of assuming. Prepare yourself for the possibility that you're right, but let her speak her mind. Perhaps it's not what it looks like." Max sounded hopeful, and I wanted to feel that optimism too, but I couldn't imagine another reason she'd be *terrified* of kids.

"I don't think it's a deal-breaker. I mean, she's the one I want to be with. Without her, kids wouldn't be a possibility."

"You mean if you stayed single." Max raised an eyebrow at me. "But what about down the road? Are you going to be my age and look back, wishing you had kids? Can you live with the potential regret? Think about all of it before you leap in. Don't go into it thinking you can change her and don't give up things that will ultimately make you miserable. That's not fair to you or her." Max looked away at a huge cloud that resembled a wild stallion, and I thought about his words for a moment.

I had no idea if I would regret this down the road. I had thought about it for a while now, but all I knew was that I wouldn't want kids with anyone else besides Miranda. If she didn't want kids but wanted me, that was all that mattered. I already jumped all-in with her, and I wasn't scared to fall. The thing I feared the most was the possibility of falling without her.

"Just prepare yourself but think things through." Max stood up, and I stood with him.

"Thank you for your wise counsel. I think you provided the clarity I needed," I said as he walked toward the sidewalk. He gave me a quick salute and headed toward my neighbor's place, whistling all the way.

I watched Max go and sank back into my chair. Picking up my beer, I took a sip and thought about everything Max had said. I was daydreaming about what my future might look like as my phone rang. A bolt of excitement flashed through me as I fished it out of my pocket. Maybe Miranda was finally getting back to me after the texts I'd sent her last night, but it wasn't Miranda calling me. It was Ethan.

Steeling myself for the worst, I answered. "Hey, what's going on?"

"I wanted to apologize for last night." Ethan's voice was even and hopeful. "Things got hairy, and I was a jerk."

I shook my head, even though he couldn't see me. He had nothing to apologize for. "No worries. I was a dick, so I had it coming."

He laughed. "Well, I won't argue with you. You weren't putting up with any shit last night, were you?"

"Nope." I took another drink of my beer, not bothering to hold back my smile. "So now, be honest with me, are you seeing anyone?"

He seemed to sober right up, his laughter gone, but it returned a moment later. "Nah."

"Are you interested in anyone?" I waved at a passing neighbor walking his cocker spaniel, and he waved back, flashing me a broad smile as he crossed the road.

"Are you kidding?" Ethan laughed. "I've been watching firsthand how miserable you are while you try to figure things out with the sheriff."

"Hey," I snapped in my best warning tone, but there was no bite behind the word. His good-natured ribbing didn't bother me.

He continued as if I hadn't said a word. "And I remember how difficult falling in love was for poor Noah. What a nightmare. You think I want to bring that kind of insanity into my life?" He let out a snort. "No, thank you. You all can take your misery and keep it to your damn selves."

That was one way to look at things, but he was missing the best part—that sense of love, of connection. There was so much more to it than misery. The misery was such a small part. "I think you're focusing on all the wrong stuff."

"Or maybe you want me to be as miserable as you are. Misery loves company or whatever." The humor in his tone put me at ease, and all was right in the world. Sure, we'd have our little spats, but we always came around in the end. We were brothers, and nothing would change that.

And no matter what anyone might tell you, there's no such thing as brothers who get along all the time.

CHAPTER NINETEEN

MIRANDA

Was it already Wednesday? I hadn't gotten back to Bayden since Saturday night. No wonder his messages were becoming progressively more worried. Around this time of year, I took time off—on call —for personal reasons.

Sinking onto my bed, I nibbled on my lip and wrote out a text.

Safe! Sorry, I'm so awful. I'm still alive, I promise. First, I'd told him not to stop by, and then I ghosted him. Great. I was a jerk. But with that olive branch text sent, I breathed a sigh of relief. It felt good to have that outside contact. With my mother's calls becoming an almost daily thing, talking to someone else was nice.

You're not awful. I know you're going through some stuff. I'm here if you need me.

He was so darn sweet. I wanted to hug the phone, hoping he'd feel it, as stupid as that was. *Thank you. You have no idea how much I appreciate that.*

You're very welcome. How are you?

I tensed up. I couldn't help the involuntary reaction. What could I tell him? I wasn't okay. Not by any stretch of the imagination. I also didn't want to worry him or stress him out. I typed out my response and sent it. *I've been better, but I'm surviving.*

Sometimes surviving is all you can do. That's enough for now.

I smiled. *So how has work been?*

Good. Missing you, though.

Missing you, too.

My texting screen disappeared, replaced by an incoming call. My heart sank as I stared at the number. I didn't know if I had the emotional energy or grit to get through another one of her rants, but what choice did I have?

I answered the call, and before I lifted the phone to my ear, I could hear her wailing. "She's gone! She's gone, and it should have been you."

I closed my eyes and saw my sister's face on the other side of my lids. After everything I'd been through, I could get through this too. Still, all the calls, the accusations, and the hatred wore me out.

"Don't ignore your mother." My father's shout elicited a flinch from me, and my eyes flew open. "She's right, you know. You were irresponsible and now we can never get her back. I'm not sure how you can live with yourself."

My chest compressed so tightly I couldn't breathe. "Some days, I wish it had been me."

The second I said the words, I knew I shouldn't have. My mother screeched like a mouse being scooped up by an eagle, and my father bellowed nonsense.

And something in me snapped. "I wish it had been me, so I don't have to go through this every time you guys have your mental break-downs. I wish I were the one, so I don't have to be your freaking punching bag." The words felt good flying from my lips, and the sounds they made only added to my sense of relief. I'd never stood up for myself before.

"Maybe, Mom, if you and Dad weren't so busy going out partying and hadn't left a nine-year-old to watch a six-year-old, Alisa would still be alive right now!" How long had it been since I said her name?

My father spluttered as if someone was holding his head underwater, and he was fighting for air. But my mother let out a thin, keening wail that pierced right through me.

"No, you killed her!" My mother's broken words had no power anymore.

"No, you left a young child to watch a younger child without an adult. *You killed her.*" I was done taking the blame. I was done being the one they despised and beat down. They were responsible. They were the ones investigated for negligence. The only reason I stayed in their home as a small child was because I had begged to, hoping I could heal them.

"I didn't know that swimming in the creek might lead to something horrible. I was nine! How could I have stopped her? What did you expect me to do? Lock her in the house?" She could have unlocked the door and left, anyway. I had no authority over her; I barely had control over myself.

"You were supposed to watch her!" My mother's howl sent a shiver down my spine.

I remembered the fear in my sister's eyes as the water grabbed her, and her feet swept from under her. I ran alongside the stream for as far as I could, branches clawing at my hair, blackberry bushes scratching my arms and legs, stinging pain, and burning lungs. I raced as fast as my legs could carry me, trying to stay with her.

I dove in the water after her as she floated, caught in an eddy that turned her in a slow circle in a still pool of ice-cold water. So cold, the chill seeped into my bones and stayed there. My fingers shook as I tried to wake her, but she wouldn't move. I stood there with her, waiting for her to wake up, but she didn't.

And the neighbor that found us had asked where our parents were. She tried to pry me from Alisa, but my hands felt frozen into fists around my sister's shirt. I couldn't answer her questions, because I didn't know.

There were bright lights and the hospital and asking the doctors if my sister had woken up. What haunts me is the look they gave one another. At the tender age of nine, I knew then that my sister hadn't woken up, and she never would. She was gone.

Sometimes surviving is all you can do. That's enough.

But was it enough?

"It was your job to keep her safe!" I wasn't sure if my mother's words were over the phone or in the hospital room all those years ago. They were the first thing she'd hissed at me when the doctors finally left the room.

They had hooked her up to all kinds of wires and beeping machines. I was confused, aching, scared, and more alone than I'd ever felt. Even at that age, I knew my sister wouldn't be coming home ever again. I'd learned that because my great grandma had passed not long before and she'd never come back. My parents had explained that she was in a box under the ground, but that it was just her body. What made her the woman I loved was gone.

What made my sister who she was, was gone.

Something inside me was missing too. A piece of me was buried with her.

"You hear me? Don't you turn this around on me!" My mother's low, growling voice filled my ear, and I glanced around my bedroom, grounding myself in the moment as the memories faded—memories I'd never allowed myself to think about. Thoughts that held me prisoner to the woman and man who made my life hell.

They weren't my parents. Parents helped their children; they loved them and worked through tragedies together. No, my parents died that day with my sister, and so did I.

"I'm done with this. Done with your lies and accusations. Take responsibility and ... never call me again." I pressed the end call button and stared at the screen until it went dark. Had I said all those things to her? Had I hung up on her? Had I stood up for myself?

Why don't I feel better?

Somehow, I felt worse than before. Mom needed to blame someone and accusing me was the only thing that got her through all this time without my sister. I'd stolen that away from her. I placed the blame directly on her shoulders. What if she did something rash? How would I ever forgive myself?

What if she came looking for me? I destroyed her, why wouldn't she seek to ruin me? The first person who would approach them was Benji. A shiver trickled down my spine at the thought of Benji having my life story. I thought about my secret being blown wide open, being out there for everyone to read. How could anyone trust me to serve and protect when I couldn't do that for my family?

In my imagination, everyone looked at me with pity in their eyes. I would no longer be the strong woman I fought so hard to become. I'd be forced to run again.

My throat closed up, and tears stung my eyes. I didn't want to run because I loved the people, loved the town, loved my life ... all but the part where my parents were in it.

My heart thumped painfully in my chest as I pondered what to do next. Maybe I could call back, smooth things over. It was a thought, but I knew there was no way I could endure a moment more of her abuse.

This time of year wasn't about me; it wasn't about my mother. It was about Alisa, my sister, and her loss and our sorrow. We should have pulled together and become tighter than ever because of this tragedy.

Instead, they'd blamed me. Ruined my life as best they could.

Broken and exhausted, I flopped back on my bed and stared at the ceiling as emotions washed over me. All I thought about was Bayden.

I know you're going through some stuff. I'm here if you need me.

I needed him, but I didn't have the mental strength to explain what I was going through, so I curled on my side and let my memories take me away.

A chill swept through me as I stood there at the edge of the water. The first step was icy. Tingling hot like fire. The second step squeezed the breath from my lungs as I focused on her still form lazily spinning in circles.

Her snowy skin seemed too pale, and I wasn't sure why she wasn't moving. She could swim out now, so why wasn't she? The cold enveloped my body, and goosebumps broke out up and down my arms.

One step at a time. I felt the current tug, but gently, playfully, almost. I reached for my sister, afraid to touch her. I grabbed her shirt, ready to pull her out of the water, but something held me there. I couldn't move as I studied her, her brown eyes wide open and staring at the sky. Frozen, I stood stiffly, waiting for something. I didn't know what that was, but I couldn't move.

"Alisa?" I whispered.

The only noise was the slight tinkling sound of the water splashing over the rocks. Numbness crept through me, slowly overtaking me until I felt nothing. Not my body. Not my fear. Not my sense of self-preservation. I felt nothing.

Blackness washed over me, drowning everything else out.

CHAPTER TWENTY

BAYDEN

I didn't understand where things had gone wrong. We'd been doing so well, chatting a bit via texts, and then ... radio silence. She sent me the all safe message, but my gut told me something wasn't right, and she hadn't responded since that brief conversation.

I'd love to see you again soon. Ugh, I sounded like a desperate teenage boy.

Pacing back and forth in my kitchen while my dinner burned on the stove, I stared at my phone and waited for her response, but none came.

I can bring pizza again and beer this time. My hopeful feeling was fading quickly. *Worried about you. Please let me know you're okay.*

The acrid smell of smoke tickled my nose, and I set my phone on the counter to pull the pan off the burner. The pork seared to the pan, hopelessly stuck and smoking. I dropped the whole thing in the sink, promising myself I'd deal with it later.

With my stomach grumbling, I looked inside the fridge before pulling out something simple like salad fixings.

I put a bowl on the counter, then checked my phone. Nothing. Not a call, not a text, no response at all—zilch.

I washed my hands, then rinsed the romaine and tore it up. The visceral ripping of lettuce calmed me somewhat, but fear roiled up in my gut. *What if something is wrong?*

I wanted to drop everything, hop in my truck, drive to her place, and make sure she was all right, but she'd told me not to do that.

Adding some mushrooms to my salad, I diced the tomatoes and scraped them off the cutting board into the bowl. Pulling open the fridge door, I reached for the leftover chicken I'd grilled the day before and grabbed the ranch, all the while thinking about Miranda.

I thought about her text.

Thank you. You can't know how much I appreciate that.

She appreciated that I was there for her. That meant that whatever was going on, whatever reason she'd gone suddenly quiet, it wasn't me, right?

I shredded the chicken with my fingers and tossed the bits into the bowl on top of the lettuce. Something else must have happened. But what, and why not tell me? That was the part that drove me nuts. It's not like I'd use whatever she was going through against her, and I'd never given her a reason to believe I'd do something so awful.

Maybe there is somebody else. I only entertained that thought for a second; she wasn't like that. She would have made it clear if she were interested in someone else. Washing my oily fingers with warm soapy water, I wondered what could have caused her to stop messaging me so abruptly. Whatever it was, it had to have been significant.

Going back to my salad, I added salted sunflower seeds for crunch, dried cranberries for sweetness, and a light helping of ranch dressing.

When my salad was finally done, I grabbed my phone and went and sat on the couch, staring at the wall and shoving bites of lettuce into my mouth.

When she'd responded the way she did, I thought we turned a

corner. I was sure things would be different. I scrolled back through the messages, searching for something that might have made her non-responsive, but everything seemed fine. I was supportive, kind, and not pushy. Overall, I was a good friend slash boyfriend or whatever I was.

Is everything okay? You disappeared.

I sent the text before I could change my mind and took another bite. Maybe I annoyed her and had come on too strong. I probably needed to back the hell off and leave her alone until she came to me. That would be the smart thing to do. Heck, that might even be the right thing to do. I didn't know anymore. I couldn't seem to get through to her, and that killed me. And every time her walls seemed ready to crumble, she fortified her emotional fortress.

The urge to call became overwhelming, and I dialed her number. Swallowing my food—despite not having chewed nearly enough—I choked down the bite, feeling the stinging scratch of sharp sunflower kernels tearing down my throat, lubricated by the ranch that made it burn all the more.

When she didn't answer, I didn't know what to do. I just sat there helplessly, trying to ignore the pain I'd stupidly caused myself.

I picked up my phone again and dialed, but this time—not knowing who else to turn to—I called Noah.

"Hey, Bay." Noah's calm voice and the sound of him gently telling Kandra he'd take the baby brought a smile to my face. "Everything okay?"

"Not really, no." I didn't know how to tell him everything that was going on. As much as I needed communication, I wasn't the best at it myself. I was better at it than Miranda, but only somewhat.

"How can I help?" My brother's easy tone calmed down the uncertainty raging within me.

"It's about Miranda. I know she's going through something serious, but she won't let me in, I don't know how I can help, and it's freaking killing me." The words poured out, and Noah let out a chuckle.

"I'm not laughing at you. I remember that feeling."

Noah knew better than most what I was saying. After all, Kandra hadn't told him she was pregnant for a long time. He knew what it was like to be with someone dealing with challenging life stuff but wasn't forthcoming about it.

"Okay, well, I assume you've tried texting and calling." Noah got right down to business as Kip made soft cooing sounds.

"I have, and there's been no response. We were texting, and we talked, but then she dropped off the map and nothing since." Again, that sense of unease rose in me.

"And this was when?"

"This afternoon." I breathed a sigh of relief. My brother would have some ideas about what we should do. He always had advice to give.

"And you're sure she's not working, that she didn't have something else to do?" Noah's calm infiltrated my thoughts.

"She's on a mini-vacation." That also rubbed me wrong. She wasn't the type to take time off. She loved her job, and it was everything to her. I mean, I get that some people have to get away from their jobs, but not Miranda.

"So, not at work then. Hmmm. Have you tried going out to her place?" Noah's innocent question earned a shake of my head as I shifted on the couch next to my forgotten salad.

"No, she told me not to come without her permission."

"Sheesh, what did you do to make her say that?" Noah asked, and Kip cried as if startled by the sudden noise.

"Serves you right." I waited for him to calm the baby before responding. "She told me to respect when she needs space."

"That makes sense. I mean, we both know that she's an independent, self-possessed woman." The pride in his voice matched the pride I felt.

"Yeah, she is, and I love that about her." I hoped he wouldn't notice my slip, and if he did, he wouldn't say anything about it.

"Well, it sounds like the best thing you can do for her is to let her be. Sorry, brother, relationships are never easy." Noah's gentleness soothed some of my frustration.

"I can't shake the feeling that she's in trouble, or that she's in a terrible place, you know?" I hated the fact that if something had happened to her, I'd never forgive myself. Maybe something had happened with her sleep issue.

"If you think she's in danger, call the deputy."

I shook my head, again, even though he couldn't see me. "She'd never forgive me if I was overreacting." Did the deputy even know about her sleeping problem? She was such a private person, and I couldn't imagine anyone knowing anything about her they didn't have to know.

"That's a fair concern. One you need to balance against other options. Is it a hunch she's not okay? Or do you know something that leads you to believe she's not okay?" He was dancing around, not coming right out and asking me, and I appreciated that he gave me some space to talk without telling him anything.

"Like I said before, she's been going through some stuff. She wouldn't hurt herself, but she has some things that make me worry." That was vague enough I felt comfortable saying the words.

"Do you think if you showed up, she'd lose her mind?"

I lifted my shoulders. "Well ... she asked me not to show up unannounced, and I am worried I'd be crossing a line if I did after she was so clear." There was no right answer.

"Do you think she'd be less angry if you told her you were worried about her because of the things you know about her?" Noah's careful wording put me at ease.

"I don't know. I'm not sure she'd be fond of me pointing it out or bringing it up, but maybe it would help her be a little less mad." Would she forgive me if I deliberately went against what she said?

"Look, the one thing I've learned from everything Kandra and I went through is that you need to communicate. You need to talk about everything. You need to tell her your concerns and fears. I'm not telling you to go against her wishes, but I am saying you two need to talk." As my brother spoke, Kip cooed as if he was part of the conversation and the little noises warmed my heart.

I struggled with what to do next. Did I show up at her place, full of concern about her well-being? I trusted my gut and always had. It never let me down before. As a sheriff, she'd understand that better than most people, right? Could she fault me for caring enough to want to make sure she was okay?

"I'm sorry there are no simple answers. I don't envy you or this sticky situation you're in, brother." Noah made a slight noise, and I knew he was entertaining Kip.

"Thank you for everything," I said.

I knew what I needed to do. I needed to check on her.

CHAPTER TWENTY-ONE

MIRANDA

I woke up with my heart pounding in my throat. I glanced around my living room, searching for whatever was responsible for dragging me out of my exhausted slumber. After the fight with my mother, I hadn't had a second of peace.

My phone.

My gaze found it on the coffee table. Maybe that had woken me up. I thought I'd set it to silent, but my mind was so muddy and jumbled I couldn't be sure of anything.

A knock at my front door sent my pulse racing, and I leaped up off the couch and stared at the front of my home. Had my parents found me already? How? I didn't doubt my mom and dad would look for me, especially now, but I thought I'd have more time.

It wasn't a pounding knock like I'd expect from my angry family, though.

Tiptoeing to the front door, I peeked out the peephole.

Bayden stood on the other side, ruffling his hair with one hand and looking side to side as if I was hiding in the bushes in the front yard to mess with him.

What is he doing here? Unlocking the deadbolts one by one, I opened the door. His gaze met mine, and the relief in his features filled me with warmth.

"Miranda." He stepped toward me, and I threw myself into his arms. I could be upset, but I wasn't. I needed his hugs and his warmth.

"Are you okay?" he asked in a soft, worried voice.

I shook my head, clinging tighter to him as all the pain and misery of the last couple of weeks—and my ability to hold it back—stretched to a breaking point. Tears streamed from my closed eyes as I inhaled his scent—fresh laundry and cedar.

He pulled back and looked me in the eyes as if he could mend my brokenness with his stare. Then he softly brushed my hair back from my face and sighed.

"You look like you haven't been sleeping. How long has it been since you ate?"

His sweet concern nearly broke me.

"I'm not sure." *How long had it been since I last ate?*

"Do you have anything here, or should I order something?" He held on to me, his hands strong as he gripped my hips.

"I, uh…" All the turmoil in my life had turned everything upside down. I didn't know what day it was, let alone the minor details like what was in the fridge.

Without a word, Bayden scooped me up in his arms, carried me to the couch, and laid me down. Pulling a blanket over me, he kneeled, kissed my forehead, and smiled before speaking. "I'll look around, and if I don't find anything, I'll order something. No worries, okay?"

I nodded, mute as that painful lump backed up my throat. "I can take care of it," I whispered.

"I know you can." He thumbed a tear from my cheek. "But I want you to know that with me around, you don't always have to. Everybody needs help sometimes, but that doesn't make you weak, it makes you human." With that, he quickly brushed his lips against mine, stood up, and walked off, leaving me thinking about how perfect he was for me ... except for that one thing.

He was back within a few moments and sat down at the end of the couch near my feet. With an absentminded touch, he rubbed my leg while speaking up. "Food will be here soon."

"Were you trying to text?" I asked. I felt awful because I told him we had a system, and then I'd blown everything.

He nodded.

"I'm sorry. I'm just..."

I trailed off as he shook his head. "I don't want to be another point of stress. I know you're coping with some things, and I'm sorry for showing up unannounced, but I wanted to be here for you." His throat bobbed as he swallowed, and I knew it had been a struggle for him to make this call.

Maybe I was a bit annoyed that he had shown up, but given that we set these rules for me texting, I was okay because I didn't follow the rules either. I blamed myself, not him. "I want to talk about it, I do ... but I never have."

I needed him to understand, even though I also knew it probably made little sense.

"When you're ready, we'll talk. Until then, I'm going to make sure you're safe and fed." He smiled at me, and my heart danced in my chest. Bayden Lockhart was freaking amazing.

"This is a rough time of year for me." The words seemed to ease the crushing pressure inside me. He didn't say a word, and I was grateful for his silence. "It's not that I don't trust you, I've just ... held this in so long it feels impossible to let it go."

"You don't have to explain anything to me." He gave my leg a quick rub, then stood up as someone knocked on the door. I watched him over the back of the couch and saw him open the door to Ethan, who pushed a big Tupperware bowl into his hands, gave him a quick around-the-shoulder hug, then turned and left.

Bayden walked into the kitchen while I imagined what it was like to have a family I could just call to bring me food—people who'd drop everything and help when I asked for it. I stood up and moved into the kitchen to find Bayden ladling soup into two bowls.

"My brother made this yesterday for a family thing. I figured he wouldn't mind sharing, and it seemed perfect for the moment." He turned to me with a bowl of steaming chicken noodle soup.

My mouth watered at the hearty aroma, and I smiled. "I'm so jealous of your family. You guys love each other so much." He had no idea how lucky he was, but I knew.

We settled onto the couch and ate. "Have you been out to the old farmhouse?" I missed our little game of cat and mouse out there.

He shook his head. "It's not as much fun right now for some reason." His gaze met mine, and I knew he was saying that I was part of his enjoyment in going out there.

"Oh, I see." I couldn't hold back a smirk.

My phone lit up, and instantly, the hair on my body stood on end. Terror zinged up my spine, and the soup on my spoon spilled into the bowl as my hands shook. Bayden was here, and that meant he wasn't the one calling or texting.

He glanced at the phone, then at me. Then, he picked up the phone, powered it down, and set it back on the table.

"It doesn't own you, you know," he whispered.

He didn't understand. How could he when I hadn't told him anything?

"You don't have to answer it, no matter who it is." He took another bite of soup before looking at me again. "You're on vacation, so even work can take a back seat. Cross Creek will survive."

He was right. Still, not answering didn't make me feel better. "This soup is amazing," I said, needing to distract myself from the uneasiness that was threatening to rise up my throat. "Please thank your brother for me."

He chuckled. "You better thank him yourself."

I smiled, instantly planning to return the bowl with something equally yummy in it when I felt up to the task. As Bayden and I talked about everything and nothing, my stress washed away like sand swept from the beach by cresting and receding waves.

I laughed at his jokes, enjoyed my time with him, and forgot the little things that would eventually tear us apart. Life began to seep back into me as if this was what I needed all along.

"When are you back to work?" he asked.

I shrugged. "Next week."

"When's the last time you got out of the house?"

I couldn't tell him, because I didn't know.

"You live out here with no neighbors for miles. Show me your favorite spot. Let's go on an adventure." His eyes sparkled, and my heart somersaulted. Now, he was speaking my language.

TEN MINUTES LATER, we dressed for the fall chill in the air and headed out the door. The trail I used was overgrown but still visible, and I inhaled the crisp snap of the breeze. All around us, trees pressed in close, some sporting green needles, while others showed off bright-yellow, red, and burnt-orange leaves.

Bayden stood beside me, his gloved hand taking mine as we pressed into the woods. The air cooled around us, and my heart lifted. Something about nature eased the burdens of life, but somehow, I'd forgotten its healing properties while I was buried in despair.

"It's nice out here," Bayden said as he gazed up at the trees. Sunlight peeked down on us and lit up the forest floor. All around, signs of life flourished from the darting squirrels to the mushrooms and chirping birds. The whole place was alive, and that vibration sent a tingle deep into my core.

"It is." I was grateful to him for coming over to get me out of my house and out of my head. "Thank you for spending the day with me."

"Thank you for sharing this with me." He smiled, then scanned the beauty around us.

"I used to hike a lot," I said wistfully, remembering how I used nature to escape from my woes.

"Why did you stop?"

I lifted my shoulders. "I'm not sure. Life got busy, and I lost my drive to get up and go. I also used to throw a tent in my old car and go on a whim. I'd stay out camping for a few nights, sleep under the stars, and sit by the campfire sipping hot coffee." He stopped and stared. "Is something wrong?" I turned to face him.

"No. We should do that. You and me. Tonight." The excitement in his face made me laugh, and then I realized he was serious.

"You're not kidding?" I cocked my head in question, and he shook his.

"Nope. Let's go back to your place, then I'll run home, and we'll pack the stuff we need to go for a night. I'll drive." His expression left me breathless. He had big, pleading eyes that somehow asked everything in their blue depths.

I nodded my head. "Let me show you this spot first, then we'll go." We started walking again, his hand still in mine as my mind whirled round and round. I'd never known anyone like him. Who else would pick up without a moment's notice and go camping with me for a night?

My pulse elevated as I realized it would be Bayden and me, sharing space beside a fire under the stars all night long. He might not know it yet, but I planned to zip our sleeping bags together and keep him close.

CHAPTER TWENTY-TWO

BAYDEN

Our night of camping had seemed to be what she needed. By morning, she looked like she'd had a good night's sleep. The dark circles under her eyes were gone, and she appeared refreshed. Her quick smile was back, and color replaced the ashen tone of her skin.

It was my first time sleeping with someone under the stars, and I teased her about her oath to uphold the law while we made love in the middle of the wilderness. Even now, I couldn't keep the damn smile off my face.

Maybe we'd turned a corner. Things finally seemed to go well for us, and I wasn't about to let her climb back into the self-imposed prison that was keeping her hostage.

Now, sitting in my truck on my way home, I thought about how she kissed me goodbye after we'd broken down our camp and respectfully cleaned up and buried the fire. She seemed sad to leave, like she never wanted our time to end, but she'd needed to get home and shower, and no doubt, I needed the same. I could smell the campfire smoke clinging to my clothes and body.

My phone rang, and my heart stuttered to the point I thought it might stop altogether. Was she calling me?

I pushed the Bluetooth headset button on the steering wheel and spoke. "Hello?"

Noah's voice had my heart settling back into place—albeit lower with dejection. "Hey, brother. I was wondering if you can take Kip for a few hours?"

"Absolutely. I'm out and about now. Want me to swing by?"

"Could you?" Noah's tired voice sounded hopeful.

In the background, I heard Kandra call out. "You're a lifesaver!"

"Sure, be there in a few minutes." I hung up and changed course, thrilled to spend some time with my nephew, though Miranda never strayed far from my thoughts.

AN HOUR LATER, Kip and I were safely in my living room. "I'm glad you like the swing." He had passed out in the car seat to music and motion. I scooped him up, careful not to wake him, and put him down. I'd transformed the guest room into a makeshift nursery, complete with crib, toy box, books, and a rocking chair. The swing was my latest purchase.

I meant it when I said I would be the world's best uncle, and I didn't doubt my other brothers would wind up with kids too, so it's not like these things would go to waste.

As the tiny boy slept, I sat down in the rocking chair, running a fingertip over the books' spines. They were all classics our parents read to us. After the beautiful time I had with Miranda, the possibility of not having kids struck me.

I refused to go into the situation thinking I could change her mind. I wouldn't be that person. I respected her wants, needs, and dreams. If those included not having children, then we'd figure it out.

The thought of having Miranda by my side was all that mattered. I loved her. Kids were great, sure, but without her, what was the point? Noah's situation taught me a lot. It didn't matter that Kip didn't share our family blood because I loved him like I'd love any other nephew or niece. Love doesn't have to look a certain way. Miranda and I could love and be happy, independent of children.

I left the nursery and my sleeping nephew to prowl around before taking out my phone to shoot her a text. *I miss you.* I hated that I was suddenly this corny human being, but it was true; I missed her already. She'd become a necessary part of my existence.

"Dad, man, I miss you. I wish you were here and could meet Miranda; she would sweep you right off your feet before you even knew what hit you." I said to the quiet room. "She is a force of nature, and I would risk anything to be with her, although there isn't much risk because it is like trying to breathe underwater without her. Being with her is what gives me life." If my father had any input, he was keeping them all to himself. I didn't mind, though.

Just the thought of her brought happiness to my heart. Being with Miranda was an adventure that I never wanted to stop taking. As she had proven yesterday, our lives were what we made of them. Her impromptu camping trips were now something I planned to continue doing with her every chance we got.

Kip woke an hour later, and I was feeding him when Kandra called. "Hey, would you be willing and able to watch him overnight? I'd like to have a date night with my husband," she asked. I knew exactly how important date nights were. "Sure. I'm enjoying my time with him." I glanced down into Kip's eyes. He furrowed his forehead and gazed at the bottle as if silently warning it not to move while he took a few breaths.

"Thank you so much. Ethan said he's also willing to watch him, so if anything comes up or you get bored, give him a call."

I snorted. "You would let Ethan watch him? Are you nuts?"

She laughed. "Good night, Bayden."

"Night." We hung up, and I set the bottle on the coffee table before lifting the baby to my shoulder. "Ethan, huh? I'm a better uncle than Ethan." Kip let out an enormous belch in response, and I chuckled.

Someone knocked at the door, and I stood up. Had Miranda

decided to spend some time with me? If so, I would scare the poor woman senseless by showing up at the door with a baby on my shoulder. Maybe she should have called first so I could have warned her. I snorted at my humor, thinking back to her stipulations. Unlocking and opening the door, I was disappointed to find Ethan on the other side instead.

"I told Kandra I've got this." I swung the door open in a clear invitation for him to follow and walked back inside. He closed the door behind himself and joined me on the couch. Offering Kip his bottle, I watched my brother's posture, noting he was sitting forward, elbows on his knees, his hands together as he studied them.

"Okay, what's eating you?"

"I'm glad you finally moved on from Angie to Miranda, but I need to know that you're actually over Angie." The raw pain in his voice surprised me.

"*Over* Angie?" I asked, confused.

Ethan seemed to reconsider before asking, "There's something between you and Angie." His statement hit me like a surprise right hook to the jaw.

Well, I knew this was going to come back and bite me in the ass someday. I sighed. "No, there isn't." The hard questions were going to follow, and I swore to answer them honestly. I wasn't going to insult my brother by screwing with him.

"Was there ever anything between you two?" Ethan stared intently at me as if he was some kind of human lie detector that would catch me if he watched closely enough.

I shook my head as Kip sighed around the bottle. "There is nothing between us and has never been anything between us."

"What's with the flirting and the weird, passive-aggressive questions?" Ethan's eyes narrowed as he rubbed the palms of his hands together without lifting his elbows off his knees.

"This is stupid." I wasn't ready to tell this story, but now was a better time than any to come clean. This had been bothering me for a while. Now that I had the chance to get it out in the open, I needed to face the truth. "Angie approached me and told me she had a crush on you. I told her to tell you. I mean, why was she telling me, right?" I lifted my shoulders, and Kip jolted awake and continued working on his bottle.

Ethan gave a slight nod, and I knew he was hanging on my every word.

"She asked me to help her out. Flirt with her. Show interest. Make you jealous so you'd come to your senses and realize you wanted her." Saying it out loud made it sound stupid and childish. Why had I ever agreed and gone along with her hair-brained scheme?

"I stopped it, though. I was tired of head games." I grinned ruefully. "It took me longer than it should have, but I realized it was a dumb ploy, and I didn't want to be part of it anymore. She begged me to reconsider, told me she thought we were close to breaking you, but I know you, man, and you're a good brother. You thought I was interested, so you backed off."

Now for the hard part. "I'm sorry for doing you like that. I was an asshole, and I should have been better to you."

Ethan lowered his head and laughed. "She wanted me so badly she tried to get you to pretend to be interested in her so I'd get jealous?"

I nodded.

"And it was *her* idea?" He glanced at me as if silently daring me to lie to him.

I nodded again.

"How the hell did she know that would bug me more than anything?" Ethan's grin lightened the weight in my chest. "It worked, you know. Thanks." He threatened to punch me in the thigh but pulled back because of the baby in my arms.

"Are you going to ask her out?" Had the ruse worked? What the hell were the odds of that?

"Wouldn't you like to know?" Ethan glared at me sideways. "If I told you, would you tell her?"

I shook my head. "Bros before ho—" I thought better of what I was saying, "—me town girls." Turning the phrase around, I watched him smile—grin, really—a big shit-eating one that took up his face.

"I think I will ask her out. I've had a thing for her for a long time." He jerked his shoulders up. "I was too much of a wuss to do anything about it. When you started paying attention to her, I figured I had waited too long and lost the chance. Now I'm glad I didn't accept that bullshit." He kicked my ankle with his work boots.

"Ow," I said on a loud sigh, glaring at him. "You're lucky I have the baby, or I'd be pummeling you on the lawn."

"Good. Pretty sure I owe you one." He flipped me off and headed for the door. "You'd lose, by the way."

He was probably right. He had a few years on me, and that added up to skill. He'd had his ass beat a few times by Noah to learn a thing or two.

"We good?" I asked as he opened the door.

"We're good." With that, he left, and I smiled down at Kip. "I hope you get to experience the joy and suffering of brothers."

CHAPTER TWENTY-THREE

MIRANDA

I watched Ethan leave Bayden's place and reminded myself I owed him some yummy treats in exchange for the delicious soup.

"Thank you for the soup," I said as he passed me. "It was amazing."

"You're welcome." He kept right on walking, and I made my way to Bayden's front door.

Gathering my courage, I lifted my hand to knock. The sound was as quick as my pounding heart, and I leaped back a step and waited.

"It's open, Ethan. What did you forget?" His voice lowered to a grumble as he pulled open the door. His face froze in shock as he stared at me, and my gut dropped to my toes as I stared at the baby in his arms.

Backing up a step, I swallowed hard, remembering why I'd come in the first place. "I'm sorry," I whispered. I shouldn't have come over without calling first. I was still riding the high of having spent the night with him, and the text he sent about missing me made me *need* to see him.

"Want to come in?" He stepped back and gestured inside.

I nodded, my legs trembling as I walked across the threshold, not taking my eyes off the sleeping baby.

"Let me put him down," Bayden said, and I nodded, sweat beading across my brow. The stumbling slams of my heart left me feeling ill, and I sank into a chair at his table while pressing my shaky hands to my thighs. I wasn't prepared for him to have the baby or for it to affect me so profoundly.

I guess that made this a better time to do what I'd planned, though. Bayden walked out, sans baby, and smiled at me. "Want a beer?"

I nodded.

He offered me one and grabbed a soda. At my curious expression, he lifted the can. "I'm still a nervous uncle and don't want to have a drop of alcohol in my system in case something goes wrong, you know?" He nodded toward the other room, and I swallowed hard, understanding his concerns.

"What's up?" His straightforward, conversational tone was what I needed.

I took a deep breath. "I'm sorry," I said again.

He seemed surprised, then hurt, and I realized he misunderstood.

"I mean, I'm sorry for all the stress and not responding to the text and for being a pain. There are things I haven't told you that you need to know." I inhaled deeply.

"I know," he said. "But I told you, you don't have to explain yourself to me."

"I want to though." Inhaling, I steeled myself for the rest. "When I was nine, my parents left me in charge of watching my sister." I fought against the memory, refusing to let it take me under. I was going to tell the story, but I would tell it on my terms, without *reliving* it.

He opened my beer, and I took a grateful gulp. He went to the fridge without a word, grabbed the six-pack, and set it before me with a nod.

Relief flooded me. Alcohol might make it easier to talk. I knew I was safe with him, no matter what happened. I wanted a clear head, though, to remember every detail of this night. So as much as I appreciated his gesture, I wouldn't take him up on it.

I fiddled with the label on the bottle, picking at it absentmindedly. "She was six and didn't see me as an authority figure, even though I was her bigger sister. She was a sassy one and had a stubborn streak that could rival a mule. We lived by a creek, not too different from Cross Creek, and she wanted to go for a swim. Although I tried to stop her, I couldn't, and she left the house and went down to the water." I took a drink, focused on a spot on the table, a swirl in the wood, refusing to let the images fill my mind's eye.

"The creek swelled from rain, so the current was faster, and the water was deeper than we were used to. The undercurrent caught her and swept her downstream, and she drowned. I stayed with her until help came." My throat closed up, and I tried to take a sip of my beer, but I couldn't swallow. I tabled the bottle, staring at it, afraid to look at Bayden.

"Can I hug you?" he asked.

I glanced at him, then stood up and threw myself into his arms. He held me tight, stroking my hair and talking tenderly to me. "Thank you for sharing that with me. What parent would think it's okay to leave a six-and nine-year-old home alone? I'm sorry you went through such a traumatic event."

His voice soothed the beasts within me, and they slumbered. I clung to him, sobs breaking from my throat as he continued to love on me wordlessly.

When I calmed down, he said, "Hey, you're strong as hell, but you didn't have to keep that inside for so long." His lips gently touched mine.

"Thank you," I whispered against his mouth.

"Thank you for opening up to me. It means a lot." His smile

warmed me up inside. "I know it was hard to do, and I'm proud of you."

For the first time in moments, I felt like I could breathe.

"Is that why you're afraid of kids?" he asked.

I nodded. "I'm just not sure I'm cut out to be a mom, you know? I'd lost one child in my life. What if I lost my own, too? I couldn't live through another loss like that."

He caught my chin between his thumb and forefinger and tilted it until we were looking at one another in the eyes. "I respectfully disagree, but if you don't want kids, then that's okay. Not having kids isn't a deal-breaker."

I pulled in a shaky breath. "You say that now, but what if you change your mind?" I fidgeted with the hem of my shirt, pulling at a stray thread until the entire bottom came unraveled.

He chuckled. "We all make choices and sacrifices. I want you more than I want kids. The outcome is the same. With or without you, there are no children in my future. That's a lot easier to swallow if I have you."

"Even if I never want to have kids?" I didn't want him hinging on some notion that I might change my mind. It was important to me to discuss it and be on the same page before we went further.

He nodded. "I've already thought about it." His gaze met mine.

My eyes opened wide. "You knew?"

"What? Your feelings about kids aren't exactly a secret."

My heart sank. I was more transparent than I thought.

"Kids aren't my primary focus. You are. I want to spend my life with you, and that isn't contingent on you popping out babies for me." He made a face. "Okay, that was crude, I'm sorry. You know what I mean."

I knew what he meant, and my heart was lighter than it had been in a long time. "I'm not saying there's no chance I'll change my mind, but I want to make sure you still want to be with me if I don't. Pressuring me to have kids later in our lives would not go well."

He nodded. "You have my word. I will never pressure you to have kids." His head lifted, and he looked down the hall. "What does this mean about my time with Kip?"

My lungs twisted, and all the air squeezed out. I couldn't live with myself if I took away his time with his nephew. "We can work something out. I don't want to come between you and your family. I can't ... you know? I can't handle the responsibility and the what-ifs."

Relief filled his features. "I understand. You've been through a hell of an ordeal, and I'm willing to do whatever it takes to work with you on it."

His words told me how lucky I was to have him in my life, and I breathed a sigh of relief that I'd come here to air the truth. "Thank you for being patient with me." Most people would not have been, but Bayden was not most people.

"I want you to be happy and comfortable, Miranda. That's all I've ever wanted." He pressed a quick kiss to my lips, and I could feel the honesty in his words.

I was a lucky woman. After a moment, I realized I was no longer shaking.

"There's more." I needed to tell him the whole truth. I took a seat in the corner chair and finished my beer.

"I'm listening," he said. "Nothing you say is going to send me running for the hills. I will always be by your side."

I smiled. "Thank you." How did he know what to say to put me at ease? "My parents ... they call me a lot. They only call to tell me that her death is my fault and that her blood is on my hands. I've heard it for over two decades, and part of me believes it. I mean ... it was my job to protect her, and I didn't."

An annoyed look settled into his eyes. "This isn't your fault. You didn't do a damn thing wrong. They did. And them blaming you ... that's insanity."

I nodded, totally agreeing with him. "That's why I left that night at the bar," I said, needing to tell him the whole truth.

"I wish I'd have known then. I would have comforted you. You know you don't have to do all of this alone, right?" He reached out and touched my knee. I stared at his hand, feeling his warmth and comfort seep into my skin and deep into my bones.

"I thought I did." It was always my burden to bear, and I'd borne it alone for so long. I had no right to put that much on someone else's shoulders.

"You thought wrong. I would have told you what nut jobs your parents are." He sat back, his hand leaving my leg. "I can't believe they blame you. It's not your fault, and you shouldn't put up with their shit."

His indignation brought tears to my eyes.

I nodded. "This is the first year I told them off."

He let out a whoop, startling me, and I jolted. "You told them off? Good job! What did you say?" He leaned in like I was getting into the good stuff.

"That they were the adults, not me. I told them it was their fault, their responsibility to keep us safe. It didn't go well. My mother lost it, and my dad is furious. They told me it should have been me and not her. Sometimes I think they're right. At least if I were gone, I wouldn't have to endure their torture any longer."

He lifted a hand. "Stop. What the hell is wrong with them? They lost one child and then just tossed you away. That's insane. You should have never listened to them."

I nodded. "I know, but my parents are broken." I didn't know how else to describe them. "I thought if I put up with it long enough, they'd come to terms with their grief and get better. This year, I realized it's only getting worse, and I'm done."

I was tired of being accused of killing my sister when I never truly got over her death, either.

"Oh, love, come here." He pulled me into his arms. "You deserved better from them. I understand you wanted to protect them, and that speaks volumes to who you are, but nobody deserves what they've put you through all these years."

I blinked as fresh tears rolled down my cheeks. My throat closed off, and I clung to him, needing his support and love. "I thought it would make a difference, but all it did was ruin me."

"Now you know better. Do you think you can focus on making a difference for yourself? For us?" His soft words spoke to some lost part of me.

"Yes. I'm ready for things to change." I was ready.

He pressed his lips to my head, and without a word, his hands stroked my back and hair.

"I love you," I whispered.

"I love you too," he answered back, his lips still on top of my head.

Finally, all was right in the world. If the peace only lasted this moment, it would go down as the best moment of my life. Bayden Lockhart loved me.

CHAPTER TWENTY-FOUR

BAYDEN

Miranda's terrified eyes met mine as she lifted her phone with shaky hands. I gave her a nod and squeezed her leg to offer strength. Side by side on the couch, we braced for what was coming. I think we both thought it was going to be unpleasant and painful, but it was also a necessary call.

For an entire week, we lost ourselves in one another. With all the love we shared, I couldn't want for more. The touching was nice, too, but the talking was cathartic. Finally, after opening up to one another, we made progress and we were officially a couple.

She confided in me about her sister and told me about her life and hellish backstory. I told her mine, though it was far less tragic.

Like a cloud, the insistent ringing of her phone had hung over us. Even with it set to silent, she constantly stared at the device, thinking about the real possibility they were calling, and they called *a lot*. A lesser person would have written them off, but Miranda cared about everyone, including two people who brought her into this world only to destroy her existence. While she loved others, she needed to learn to love herself.

She asked me to be here for her while she tried to call and reason with her parents, and I hadn't hesitated. The time had come to fix things or move on. Miranda had the power and control this time, and the decision was hers.

I wasn't sure she was ready for the outcome, but I was here for her, regardless. She exhaled before dialing and bringing the phone to her ear.

The screech at the other end of the line hurt *my* ears. "You've been ignoring my calls and texts, you ungrateful little b—"

"Mom." Miranda's calm tone halted her mother's abuse. "You need to stop and listen." Her lip quivered, but her voice didn't crack. "I know how much you're hurting, but I hurt too. It's not my fault that Alisa died. I was a child—a nine-year-old, and I should never have been tasked with keeping her safe."

I rubbed her leg, proud of her for being so calm and concise when I was so mad I wanted to shout at her harpy mother. That woman didn't deserve the title of parent.

The fear in Miranda's eyes bothered me, and I wished I could make this easier for her. I would have given anything to take the burden from her and carry it, so she didn't have to, but we both knew she needed to face them and their unfair, bullshit accusations. I couldn't do this for her, but I could support her while she waded through it. There was no way I'd let her drown in despair and guilt. Hadn't her sister's death been enough?

"You were supposed to keep her safe!" Her mother's scream tore at my heart. Despite the call not being on speaker, I heard every cruel word.

The woman hadn't healed from her daughter's death. How could she, if she never faced the truth?

"No, Mom, *you* were supposed to keep her safe. You and Dad needed to keep both of us safe. My sister was never my responsibility. She was yours." Miranda's firm refusal to take the blame for her sister's death filled me with pride. It had taken many conversations and a lot of time for her to come to terms with the truth. She didn't kill her sister. It was a tragic accident that could have been prevented had her parents been responsible. In hindsight, how could they take responsibility for the action when they didn't even take care of their kids? Some people should never be parents. Sadly, Miranda wasn't one of them. Not only had her mother and father stolen her childhood, but they stole her confidence and desire to be a mom because they'd planted a lie so deeply inside her, she believed it to her core.

"I want to move past this, though." Her hopeful tone left me praying her parents wouldn't crush her. "I want to be a family in whatever way we're able, and I think we can all heal from this if we try."

"Heal? Heal from you killing your sister?" Her mother's shrill voice radiated toxicity through the room, and Miranda's shoulders drooped. "How could we heal from what you did?"

I hated that every word out of the woman's mouth was an accusation.

"I told you, you should never have left a six-year-old home with a nine-year-old. Her accidental death is not my fault." Twin tears rolled down Miranda's cheeks, and my heart ached for her. I pulled her into a hug and let her rest against my chest. Her weight settled onto me, and I hoped she could feel me offering love and support. She deserved better than her shit parents.

"It is your fault." Her father's bellowing took over. "You should have locked the door and kept her inside!"

I rubbed her back with one hand. Every muscle in her body was taut, and she trembled in my arms. I wanted to jump in but knew that Miranda had to handle this. She couldn't gain strength from the experience if someone else solved the problem. She'd let it go on for far too long.

"I locked the door, Alisa was six, not stupid, and knew how to unlock it." Miranda had told me every detail of that day. The more she divulged, the more confident I was that the sequence of events that day was not her fault, even if her parents thought so. The bottom line was they should have never left those little girls alone. The fact that only one of their children died still stunned me. Blind luck had saved Miranda's life that day, and I was grateful to the universe for sparing her.

"Then you should have blocked her from opening the door." Her mother's voice sounded like metal being crushed.

Goosebumps covered my arms, and the tiny hairs prickled as they stood on end. One thing was for sure—I *hated* her mother.

"I tried." Miranda somehow stayed calm.

I continued stroking her back, hair, and neck, trying to rub the tension from her frame.

"You shouldn't have left us alone that day." Once again, Miranda hurled responsibility back at her parents. What was becoming evident to me was that it didn't matter what Miranda said. Her parents would never accept any blame for their part in their daughter's tragic death. Perhaps they needed to blame Miranda to get through the day like she thought, but that was no excuse. What they needed to do was accept blame, get help, and fix their lives.

I gave her a gentle pat on the shoulder, the gesture we'd agreed on if I thought the conversation was going nowhere. She nodded, silently acknowledging she felt the same. Her choices and actions were her own, but I wanted to make sure she knew how it looked from the outside. I worried that her parents would suck her back into guilt and use her as a punching bag again, and she deserved better.

"You killed your sister." Her mother's argument circled right back to the beginning, and I sighed. They were a lost cause, and Miranda needed to wash her hands of them. I'd warned her of that possibility, though I wasn't one bit happy to be right.

If her parents didn't accept that they needed help, that they could be wrong, or if they didn't want help, then there was nothing Miranda could do to fix anything. She glanced up, giving me a sad, helpless shrug, and I hugged her. Every bit of me wanted to squeeze away her pain and fix her problems. Of course, I couldn't, but I wanted to.

"I guess you're not hearing me." Miranda's sigh broke my heart. "I hope that you guys get therapy someday. I think talking to someone would help you come to terms with this loss. I'll be doing the same. One thing is for certain, I'm done letting you treat me like crap. Stop calling me to torture me, or I'm going to block your number for good."

"Miranda!" her father yelled.

Before he could finish whatever ugly statement he was about to make, Miranda hung up. When her phone lit up because they were calling back, she didn't answer. Instead, she put it on the coffee table, screen down. Her hands trembled, and her heartbeat thundered against my chest. I could feel the stress seeping out of every inch of her skin.

A moment later, she picked up the phone, powered it off, and put it back down.

"I know you were hoping for closure." I needed to speak, so she didn't sit and stew on the failure.

She let out a sad sound. "Closure is a word people use to make themselves feel better. There's no such thing. There's nothing my parents could ever say to undo what they've done or how they hurt me."

I squeezed her gently.

"Honestly, I'm grateful I can say I tried my best to fix our relationship, but how can you put back the pieces when everything is fractured beyond repair?" Her tone gave away that she wished she could have made progress. "I have to take the blame too. Not for Alisa's death, but for my part in allowing them to use me as a whipping post. When I was young, I didn't know any better, but as an adult, I should have." She chewed at her lip. "I suppose it's no different from being in an abusive relationship. You stick around and try to be perfect, hoping that things will change. It rarely does. I've seen enough aftermath of domestic abuse cases to know how it turns out. This isn't any different. Only the abusers were my parents."

"You did your best. You aired your grievances and stopped the cycle. I'm proud of you." I held her close, loving her all the more. No matter how hard I tried, I couldn't imagine having a family like hers.

What would I have done without my loving, supportive parents? Who would I have become without them and my brothers?

"Thank you," she whispered, her tears dotting my shirt.

"No matter what," I said, knowing my mother would approve of what I was about to say. As would my father if he'd been there to hear me. "You have a family now, a family that loves you unconditionally. We don't care about your past. We're focused on your future. Every single one of us, and even if you dumped me, you'll always be family." I meant every word.

Her shoulders shook as she let the emotions out. My shirt stuck to my skin because it was so wet from her tears.

"Sorry for making you cry more." I felt terrible because I'd been trying to make her feel better, not worse.

"It's okay. They're good tears." She sniffled, then let out a little laugh. With that, she sat up and turned to face me. Straddling my hips, she leaned into my body—belly to belly, chest to chest, heart to heart.

"All I ever wanted was a family." Her soft confession made me ache more for her.

"I'm sorry yours was awful. We can share mine, no matter what." I kissed her damp cheeks, then her warm forehead. Her arms wound around my shoulders, and she clung to me as if she'd never let me go.

Something whispered that this was how it was meant to be. I may have made some bold decisions in my life and not always realized all the repercussions from jumping headfirst, but my heart told me that Miranda was worth the chance. I am not worried about where we will end up because I was born to love this woman. And right now, with her in my arms, there was nothing to fear because everything was finally right in the world, and she was exactly where she belonged.

CHAPTER TWENTY-FIVE

MIRANDA

"Miranda, we've got a call about a suspicious vehicle out at the old, abandoned farm." My deputy's annoyed voice couldn't keep the smile off my face.

I knew who the suspicious trespassing vehicle belonged to.

"I'm on my way." I pointed my Tahoe toward the farm, glancing at the water bottle in surprise because it didn't pop out and roll all over the floor when I hit the first bump. I shouldn't have been shocked because Bayden had fixed the cup holder weeks ago. Still, like everything else in my life, I couldn't help but be amazed that things were working out so well.

The cup holder and Bayden and my relationship weren't the only things going better. I received a call from my mother telling me she left my father and was in therapy. He'd also gone to get help. Separately, the two of them were working on their lives, their alcohol problems, and their grief.

The call hadn't been all rainbows and sunshine—mom still held on to a lot of her anger at me, and she blamed me—but I could hear that she was seeing her contribution to the tragedy that ended my

154

sister's life. I hoped that we'd be a family of sorts one day, but I was content knowing they were getting the help they needed for now.

Who knew what the future held? I wouldn't hold my breath that my parents would ever fully come around because decades of replaying the same soundtrack had a way of changing reality. They had lied to themselves for so long they didn't recognize the truth, but I was happy for the baby steps they were taking.

In the meantime, I had a family.

Bayden's family welcomed me with open arms, and I opened up and told them my story. Their love and support surrounded me and gave me strength when I had none. My own family isolated me, but the Lockharts made me feel like I belonged.

Kandra had given me a huge hug from one side, and Irene held me from the other while Bayden rubbed my back in that absent-minded way he did that always brought me comfort.

Together we mourned my lost sister, my lost childhood, my pain, and my suffering. When we were done, we had dinner and filled the time with love, smiles, conversations, joy, and mostly laughter. The Lockharts were a bunch of jokers, and it filled my heart with glee. Bayden's family, *my family*, lifted my spirits and left me feeling more at home than I ever had.

The dirt road led me past Ethel and Norman's place, and the two waved from their front porch. I waved right back, a grin on my lips. The sly couple knew what they were doing when they called Bayden in as suspicious. Nothing could convince me otherwise, but I didn't mind one bit.

With all the changes in my life, I had things to be proud of, too, like the fact that I held little Kip. Only for a second until he started crying, and then I passed him back in abject horror that I made him cry. Kandra had been quick to tell me that it wasn't my fault and that babies sometimes cry around new people.

Her explanation made me feel better, and Kip seemed fine once he calmed back down. No injury, no lasting effects, nothing. Maybe kids weren't so scary after all. I wasn't planning to go off birth control anytime soon, but there was a glimmer of hope for a future where children didn't terrify me.

That was a good thing because Kandra confided in me that the reason she'd been so tired and leaning so hard on her brothers-in-law and mother-in-law was that she and Noah were expecting again.

No one else knew but her and Noah, so the fact that she confessed to me first had touched me deeply. She trusted me with her secret, and I resolved to be there for them this time. Which meant I needed to get over my fear of babies.

Their surprise pregnancy and the joy in her face had me over the moon for them. I'd asked if she was afraid, and she told me, of course, she was. Being a parent wasn't easy, and there was no instruction manual. You did the best you could and asked for help when you needed it.

Her words resonated with me. Had I asked for help earlier instead of hiding my pain from everyone, I may have weathered the storm more easily.

With a light heart and fresh excitement pulsing through me, I drove out to the old farm in the early morning sunshine. I'd woken up beside Bayden this morning, sad to get ready for work on his day off. He pulled me in for a kiss, then got breakfast and coffee prepared while I showered. We had found our rhythm, and it was as natural as breathing. Our time together was seamless, happy, and loving.

Avoiding the three potholes in quick succession, I enjoyed the way my heart fluttered as I thought about my life. Everything was working out better than I could have imagined. I knew there'd be hard times too, but I could handle hard times, I'd proven that over the last two decades.

With the dust kicking up behind me, I pulled in and parked beside Bayden's truck. There was no way he didn't see me coming from a mile away with all that dirt the tires brought about. I caught sight of him walking from the corner of the overgrown pasture across the drive and toward me.

When he saw me looking at him, he halted, hands up, an easy smile on his face.

With a chuckle, I opened the door and got out.

"I guess I'm busted, huh?" His sensual tone made my heart do little flips. I loved this man with everything I had.

"Yes, you are, mister." I walked toward him as he turned to stare up at the farmhouse.

"Am I under arrest?" He winked at me, and a sudden heat filled my belly.

"I haven't decided yet," I said with a teasing smirk across my face. We stood shoulder to shoulder and studied the old building for a moment.

"Talking to your father?" I asked. I knew his wounds from losing his father hadn't healed. Losing their dad had a profound effect on all the Lockharts. I often wished I could have known Kip better before he passed, but my every interaction with him had been positive. He was a good man, and that was reflected in his sons.

Bayden nodded.

"And?"

He laughed. "And what? He doesn't talk back. I think I'd need a straitjacket if he did. Despite his silence, I still hear him in my heart. Does that make me crazy?"

"Not one bit." His ability to joke gently about the topic told me everything I needed to know about his state of mind. He was in a good place, and I was happy to hear that.

"I've done something," he said, as he glanced back at the house.

Looking at the mossy roof and the caving-in corner, I almost didn't notice the beautiful lines, the intricate touches in the wood-work, and the gorgeous second-story porthole window that was a feature of the home. Even in its debilitated state, it was obvious this place had been built with love and care.

"I'm sorry I didn't discuss the decision with you first." He dug a toe into the dirt, kicking up a bit of quartz and nudging it toward the driveway's edge.

"How can I help?" It didn't matter what he did; I was in his corner for better or for worse, come hell or high water. He didn't owe it to me to discuss choices first, and I didn't need to weigh in on everything he wanted to do. We were two independent people that lived our own lives. We blended as much of it as we could. I didn't expect perfection, and I doubted he did either. Maybe it was a strange way to do things, but it worked for us.

"I bought this place." He gave me a rueful smile, then nodded toward the house again.

I glanced at him, dumbfounded.

"I'd like for us to rebuild it together."

The symbolism wasn't lost on me. We were going to take something that meant a lot to him and rebuild, like our lives.

"This was my father's secret legacy, one of his first builds and a project he loved to his dying day, and I'd like us to carry it on, to make it *our* legacy." His attention returned to the sagging roof, the rain gutters falling away from the walls, and the decaying porch.

I touched his hand. "It's still your father's legacy, and it can also be ours." Our fingers laced together, and we both held on to one another.

He studied me as I focused on the house again, imagining what it must have looked like freshly built.

"Does that mean..." He trailed off as if he couldn't voice his good fortune lest he jinxed it.

Well, I had no problem saying the words out loud. With a nod, I spoke. "I'll move in with you, and we'll rebuild this place together."

He went back to studying the house, his pulse thundering in his palm as we held hands like teenagers. "Does this mean no more harassment from law enforcement on my property? I mean, officer, do you even have reasonable cause to be here?"

I held back a laugh. "I received a call of a suspicious vehicle. It's well within my duty to follow up on that call. I'm going to need to see proof of purchase of the property." Even as I joked, I was sad that this playful part of our lives was over. All the sneaking out here, chasing him down ... I'd miss it. Knowing we were on to brighter futures helped ease the sting.

Filled to bursting with warmth and excitement, I turned to face him. We started a new chapter in our lives, the first concrete step to building one life from our two paths.

"Where do we start?" I didn't know the first thing about rebuilding houses. Lucky for me, I knew one of the best in the business, and he had three brothers.

"Want me to tell you?" he asked, giving me a sexy grin. "Or show you?"

I laughed. I wanted to see inside our home. *Our home!*

I wanted to hear his vision for the place and see him light up with joy and excitement. I couldn't help but wonder if he radiated his father's energy when he talked about building and plans.

"Show me," I said, smiling at him. "Show me everything."

He nodded his head toward Norman and Ethel's farmhouse up the road. "They knew we were perfect for each other before we did." Nothing got past the old folks in this town. They were schemers and meddlers of the best kind.

They heard everything and saw what we couldn't—that a troubled woman would find healing in a small town, a family where she had none, and love in the arms of a trespasser with a fearless heart.

SNEEK PEEK AT GUARDED HART

ANGIE

Cross Creek might hold answers to my missing father's whereabouts.

"Angie," Roy called out to me as if he had done it several times. "Where were you just then?" he asked.

I lifted both shoulders. "Sorry, I was a million miles away in my own head." Nothing had gone according to plan. I thought I'd show up in Cross Creek, extract the town's secrets, figure out if my father was here or not, then continue on my journey to find him. I didn't expect Ethan, and I certainly didn't plan on falling for him.

"Well, you might want to stop gawking at that Lockhart boy." He jerked his chin in the direction I'd been absentmindedly staring, and I followed the motion as my heart began to thunder. Ethan raised his beer in my direction with a smile before losing himself in his tablet again.

Well, this had seemed like a good idea. I figured I could work for Roy on Kandra's days off to help lighten his load.

Where do people give up secrets? Bars.

Who can someone lean on when they're having a bad day? The bartender.

Me.

I ran my fingers through my hair to smooth it down as I watched Ethan's guarded expression. He stopped touching the screen and moved the tablet back as if to take in the whole image before him, and I wondered—for the millionth time—what kept him so captivated on the darn thing. I knew technology addiction was a real thing, but sheesh.

"Take him a beer, will ya?" Roy nodded, and I sighed.

"Of course." I knew what the old man was up to and it wouldn't work. I wasn't in Cross Creek for friendship or romance. I was here for *information.*

Roy handed me a pint glass filled with chilled amber liquid. The scent of beer hit my nose, and I inhaled and wished for once I could drink without concern. Scanning the room, I made a mental note—the place was quiet for a Saturday.

Of course, Gypsy was here; she and Roy had become inseparable over the last few months. Patti waved at me, and I nodded with a smile for her. She didn't come in often, but when she did, she and Gypsy usually talked and cackled and for hours. They were generally fun to listen to and watch.

Ethel and Norman were in their own booth and every time Ethel would say something, Norman would reply with a loud "Hah?" They shared a batch of garlic knots and laughter that brought a smile to my lips as I made my way to Ethan with his beer.

Benji sat in a corner, his shoulders curled inwards as if he was in time out. The town had kind of put him there, I guessed, after his inexcusable behavior with Kandra. While Kandra had become the town sweetheart, Benji was busy trying to right his wrongs and fix his image and reputation. He'd been doing well, volunteering his time to help others and all around being a better person. Tonight, though, he wasn't alone. Some young man sat with him; a good-looking guy with blond hair, bright eyes, and an uncanny resemblance to Benji. A brother, maybe?

The stranger's gaze met mine, and he nodded. I offered a friendly smile and turned my attention to Ethan as I set his beer before him.

Something in Ethan's deep blue eyes seemed troubled, and I sat down next to him with a glance over my shoulder at Roy. The place was quiet enough I doubted he'd mind if I took a moment. Besides, Roy encouraged the small-town feel, conversation, and was a laid-back boss. It made me wonder what kind of father he'd be.

"You seem upset." I reached out and hooked a finger over the top of his tablet. Pushing the device down toward the table, I noticed his eyes narrow as they met mine. "Whatcha up to?"

"Working." His sour tone didn't faze me. I knew how grumpy he could be, and I didn't mind.

"What are you working on?" I tried to lower the tablet more so I could look at the screen, but he pulled it toward himself and pushed a button. The screen went black, and I pressed my lips together. "I want to see."

His facial features relaxed. "Really?"

I nodded and leaned in like I was sharing a secret. "I'll try not to steal your super-secret designs."

He chuckled and turned the screen back on. It flared to life, and he turned the device around. I studied the lines and measurements. Glossing over the numbers and equations, I took in the whole image. The building was beautiful.

"Is this your dream mansion on the edge of a cliff once you become rich and famous?" I smiled at him, knowing he wasn't that type of guy at all. He didn't have a flashy or show-off bone in his body —I liked that about him. Instead, he had that down-to-earth charm that warmed up my insides like hot cocoa on a snowy winter day.

He shook his head and glanced over his drawing. "No, this one's for fun."

"You could give Frank Lloyd Wright a run for his money." I studied the image again, loving the high roofs, the glass features, the beautiful angles. It might only be a sketch, but in my mind's eye, I could imagine the absolute modern palace the finished building would be.

He lit up. "What makes you say that?"

I inhaled, trying to put my thoughts into words. "Well, Frank Lloyd Wright was a visionary, an incredible architect, and he changed the way we live and build. And this," I touched the edge of his tablet, "is world's better than anything of his I've ever seen."

Ethan's eyes danced with pleasure, and a smile tugged his lips. All the shadows in his expression faded, and his eyes crinkled at the corners with pleasure. "Thank you," he said in a soft voice.

"You're very welcome... but I meant every word. So how have you been?" I wanted to know more, and having his undivided attention like that was intoxicating.

"Good, good. My brothers are all busy now that they've found love." He chuckled, but I sensed some shred of honest bitterness. Maybe he was upset he hadn't found anyone yet.

I wished I could talk about my family. It was a distant dream, however; my mother and I weren't on speaking terms since she—

My eyes stung, and I blinked quickly. I wasn't going to think about that. "You'll meet someone... if you haven't already." I couldn't think about that, either. I liked Ethan—a lot. Still, I wasn't here to find love, and I needed to keep my head on straight. I needed answers, and I couldn't slow down for love until I knew the truth.

With that, I stood up and headed toward the counter once more. No need to upset Roy and get myself into trouble. The second I locked eyes with Roy, I knew I needn't have worried; Roy's huge smile told me he was thrilled.

I liked the man, but did I really want to find out I was his daughter? All the information I'd gleaned seemed to point to him as the most likely suspect.

The thought made my heart heavy, and I smiled back at him. I'd spent so much time building relationships with everyone in town that I could. I'd been doing everything possible to dig into people's pasts without drawing too much suspicion. Somehow, I still had no answers. The things I'd uncovered seemed to point to Roy, though, and I'd been wrestling with that possibility since I'd discovered it.

As I hesitated, Roy gestured for me to go back to Ethan's table.

Why not? I turned back and the young man from Benji's table appeared at my elbow. "Hey," he said in a low voice.

"Hello," I said, friendly as always. My mind wasn't on this stranger; it was on the heavy topic that had been pushing to the front of my mind for months. I needed to figure out who my father was. I needed to know who I was and where I came from.

"Can we get a couple more beers?" He glanced back at Benji, who was still hunched forward, head down, looking beaten by the world.

"Sure." I turned back to Roy as the guy grabbed my arm right above the elbow. Offering a friendly and confused smile, I turned to face him once more. "Did you need something else?"

"What's a girl like you doing working in a dump like this?" His serious expression told me this was an honest attempt to hit on me using the weakest pickup like I'd heard in a long time.

"I happen to like this dump," I said with a soft laugh. Part of me felt bad for the guy; clearly, flirting wasn't his strongest suit. Since I wasn't the type of girl to bring anyone down, I decided to be nice instead. "But thanks." I understood his sentiment, even if I didn't agree. To someone who didn't know the town, this place might look like a total dive. I wasn't going to excuse his rudeness, but I could understand his error.

"Well, if you're ever in Silver Springs, hit me up." He offered me his number on a napkin, and I took it, stunned.

"I didn't know people still wrote numbers down," I blurted out, then covered my awkward omission by taking out my phone. "I'll put your number in now; what's your name?"

"Clark."

I keyed in his name and number, then thanked him. "It's great meeting you, Clark. Thanks." I gestured with my phone to indicate I was thanking him for his number, then headed back to the bar to grab him and his friend a drink. Hurrying to drop them off at the table, I made polite small talk without thinking about it. In my mind, I was back to thinking about how my mother had lied to me about everything.

She'd told me that my father died in the war, that he was Native American, that I was tribe royalty... so many lies stacked on mistruths and covered with misdeeds. I didn't hate my mom, but she'd made my life more difficult with her dishonesty. I'd only discovered the truth when I took a DNA test to trace my heritage and found I was not Native American at all. And as usual, she stuck to her lies when I questioned her. She'd told me the test was wrong, that they'd swapped the results, or the people who sent the results had lied.

"Call me," Clark said as I left the table. I nodded, knowing full well I had no intention to call the guy, and headed back toward Ethan's table.

That wasn't even the worst of my mother's lies... but it was all I was prepared to deal with.

Ethan was back on his tablet. "You know, you work an awful lot. Would it kill you to take some time off?" I smiled at him.

He seemed oddly upset as his gaze met mine.

"Uh-oh, I know that look. What's on your mind?" I sat back down, but he shifted, moving his body away from me in an obvious gesture that stung.

"First my brother, now someone else?" He nodded at Clark, who seemed to be watching us.

"What?" I didn't understand what he was getting at. My head seemed to be filling with cotton fluff, as if the stress of the last few months was catching up with me.

He took a deep drink of his beer, then set the empty glass down with a thud. "I'm tired of being chosen last."

What he was saying clicked. He was upset I'd gotten Clark's number. How could I tell him I was just being nice? That I had no intention of ever calling the guy? That I wasn't interested in the person who'd used the worst pickup line in history on me? Then again, why did I have to explain myself anyway? It's not like Ethan had ever asked me out. We weren't dating; I was free and clear to see whomever I damn well pleased.

The emotions of the last several months overflowed, and I lashed out. "I've always chosen you first, Ethan. Maybe your head's been too buried in your tablet to notice."

"Why did you come to Cross Creek?" His serious gaze and the gravity of the question stopped me up short.

I wasn't going to be my mother and lie, but I needed to be careful how I answered. "I came here looking for something." No way I'd tell him the whole truth. Not yet. I wasn't ready.

GET A FREE BOOK.

Go to www.authorkellycollins.com

OTHER BOOKS BY KELLY COLLINS

An Aspen Cove Romance Series

One Hundred Reasons

One Hundred Heartbeats

One Hundred Wishes

One Hundred Promises

One Hundred Excuses

One Hundred Christmas Kisses

One Hundred Lifetimes

One Hundred Ways

One Hundred Goodbyes

One Hundred Secrets

One Hundred Regrets

One Hundred Choices

One Hundred Decisions

One Hundred Glances

One Hundred Lessons

One Hundred Mistakes

Cross Creek Novels

Broken Hart

Fearless Hart

Guarded Hart

Recipes for Love

A Tablespoon of Temptation

A Pinch of Passion

A Dash of Desire

A Cup of Compassion

The Second Chance Series

Set Free

Set Aside

Set in Stone

Set Up

Set on You

The Second Chance Series Box Set

Holiday Novels

The Trouble with Tinsel

Wrapped around My Heart

Cole for Christmas

Christmas Inn Love

Mistletoe and Millionaires

Up to Snow Good

Wilde Love Series

Betting On Him

Betting On Her

Betting On Us

A Wilde Love Collection

The Boys of Fury Series

Redeeming Ryker

Making the Grade Box Set

ABOUT THE AUTHOR

International bestselling author of more than thirty novels, Kelly Collins writes with the intention of keeping the love alive. Always a romantic, she blends real-life events with her vivid imagination to create characters and stories that lovers of contemporary romance, new adult, and romantic suspense will return to again and again.

For More Information
www.authorkellycollins.com
kelly@authorkellycollins.com

Printed in Great Britain
by Amazon